Tainted Harvest

Nancy Smith

True events, people and locations inspired this book. It is impossible to know exactly what happened, but as much as possible, this story is based on the historical record. This is the author's interpretation and much of the detail is fictionalized.

Tainted Harvest

Author: Nancy Smith
Printed in the United States
Published 2016, First Look Publishing (Austin)
www.nancysmithwriter.com
Version 1.2
ISBN: 978-0-9913907-5-5
Cover Photo: Brian Burrowes
Edited by: Kirkus Editing
Printed by CreateSpace, a DBA of On-Demand Publishing, LLC

Acknowledgments

The following people greatly and graciously donated their time and expertise in reviewing this novel: Polly Enders, Leslie Hudson, Barbara Smith, Nichola Shore and the Right Rev. Dena Harrison. My thanks to them.

'It is the prerogative of the God of truth, to know all the truth in all things at once and together: It is also his glory to conceal a matter,' Prov. 25.2. And to bring the truth to light in that manner and measure, and the time appointed, as it pleaseth him; it is our duty in all humility, and with fear and trembling to search after truth, knowing that secret things belong to God, and only things revealed belong to us...

John Higginson
Pastor of the Church of Salam
March 23, 1697

As printed by:
John Hale
Modest Inquiry Into the Nature of Witchcraft
Pastor of the Church of Christ in Beverly
1697

CENTRAL SALEM HOUSEHOLDS IN 1692

PARRIS HOUSEHOLD

The Reverend Samuel Parris (38)
Elizabeth Eldridge Parris (38)
       Thomas Parris (11)
       Elizabeth (Betty) Paris (10)
       Susannah Parris (5)
       Abigail Williams (11) - Niece

Slaves:
John Indian (32)
Tituba Indian (30)
       Violet (2)

GRIGGS HOUSEHOLD

Dr. William Griggs (71)
Rachel Hubbard Griggs (69)
       Elizabeth Hubbard (17) - Great Niece

PUTNAM HOUSEHOLD

Thomas Putnam Jr. (40)
Ann Carr Putnam Sr. (31)
       Ann Putnam Jr. (12)
       Plus eleven others

Servant:
Mercy Lewis (19)

1

Orinoco Delta, August 1674

I played naked in the mud with my younger sisters Yessi and Aya. We covered our skin and hair with painted patterns made from the wet earth. As it cracked and dried, we lay on the riverbank and stared overhead. In the variegated green of the jungle cap, monkeys twittered and howled. The enormous trees were crowded with foliage and twisted with ropes of vine.

Mother waved as she walked toward us down a narrow path. We washed away the cracked mud at the edge of the river, somehow making ourselves clean and new and examined the design the sun's burning rays had made on our skin. Aya, little more than a baby, had made random lines on her naked body. She giggled in happiness at her result. Yessi needed almost all her fingers to count her years. She had made a sun with its outstretched rays in the middle of her chest. My mud painting was meant to be complex and meaningful, a portrait of a Zemi, one of our ancestrial spirits, but it turned out to be no pattern at all.

Mother smiled as she rinsed away a bit of mud left on Aya's forearm. She handed us flat bread made from yucca flour that we ate as we climbed a tall hill. We looked down over the round huts made of sticks and palm leaves that filled our small clearing at the edge of the jungle. These houses were made strong to withstand high winds and rain by sinking wooden posts into the ground in a circle and weaving canes between them with creeping vines. The roof was thatched with palm leaves. One hole at the top allowed smoke to escape.

The camp was close to a small finger of the Orinoco River, but far enough away to be out of crocodile territory and away from the bog. The tribe stayed on the savanna at this time of year.

From our small mesa, we could also see that there were warriors unknown to us floating down the river in their dugout canoes. The warriors pulled to shore. There were two who I could tell were Carib even from this distance and one man whose skin had no color at all. I had heard stories of these pale men, but had never seen one myself. I glanced at Mother and she looked curious as well.

We hid ourselves from view. We observed that several of our warriors carried bows and arrows. They followed the men to discover their purpose. We knew that the Carib could be unpredictable, sometimes menacing, sometimes deadly.

When our warriors returned to the village, their stories of the Carib were not of a threat, but of traders. Our warriors showed us a spearhead and some fishhooks that they traded for one of their bows. They said the traders had many useful items, many tools made of iron, items the likes of which most of us had never seen before. With excitement in their voices, our warriors told us tales of shiny knives and iron pots. We marveled at the practicality of such things.

My uncle leaned toward me. "I traded for a tool called scissors, two blades that pass each other to cut." He snapped the two small blades apart and together a couple times. He dramatically lifted a leaf from the ground and held it between the blades and with a smack cut the leaf in half. "They had one scissors that had a pattern of vines and birds on its handle. Very pretty. You would like."

I wanted scissors. They looked useful for cutting yarn or making baskets.

That night, the tribe communed around the fire. Many

of the warriors who had traded with the Carib wore paint and feathers. From the knees to the feet, they covered themselves in shells. This marked the ceremony as special.

The shaman, who was our mystical leader, presented a large, carved zemi figure to the cacique who was our tribal leader, our chief. The cacique sat on a wooden stump in a place of honor with the carved representation of the deity on its own pedestal in front of him. Carving the likeness of the Zemi, the God, into the stone infused the spirit of the Zemi God into that zemi object. This kept the protection close at hand.

The shaman was the tribe's eldest and most wise. His back curved like a twig in the wind, bending so far his face was nearly touching the crackling fire. He sang a song that came from deep in his chest. The song was about his animal spirit, the monkey.

The monkey acted as a guide between humans and animals. The monkey was clever and resourceful. The monkey used his hands to imitate rodents and birds in the trees, only the monkey was smarter.

My sister, Yessi, sat next to me and sang along in her beautiful, high, clear voice.

When the song was finished, my uncle started the beating of a drum.

The shaman began to tell one of the old stories we had heard many times before. "Good and wise people lived in the sky place. They never died. There were no clouds, no wind. There was just the yellow light. The grandfather lit everything from the top down to the earth. Because of that light, all his children were happy."

My father listened closely to learn the wisdom of the ancient shaman. When Father was wise with age, he would be the next shaman for the tribe. Father macerated the ceremonial leaves and vines together as the shaman spoke.

"The grandfather wanted to create spirits on the earth. He sent a messenger who brought knowledge and song, but one spirit was born different from the others. The messenger cut the rotted afterbirth and buried it. Worms ate the afterbirth and it infected some creatures with an ugly darkness. Because of them, we suffer hunger, sickness and war."

My youngest sister, Aya, cried out and my mother immediately circled her up and held her in protective arms. Aya fed from Mother's breast until she fell into a deep loose-limbed sleep. Aya was no longer hungry, but the rest of us were. It had been a horribly difficult year and we needed more food for the tribe.

Yessi and I squatted together on the ground. Yessi was fascinated by the progress of a worm toward the cooking fire. I waited for Yessi to save the worm from its fate and soon enough she did.

Yessi's animal guide was the pink river dolphin. The dolphin could change shape into a man to protect fishermen who had fallen into the water. In their changed shape, the dolphin-man would float the fallen on the tide to transport the near-drowned to shore and then would transform back into a dolphin. Yessi, too, swam like a dolphin and she had a beautiful spirit of giving.

I carefully watched as Father combined the leaves and ground them with a sharp shard. He added the leaves one by one into warm water in a gourd. He sprinkled a bit of sea salt. "For just a touch of flavor," he said with a sly smile and a wink to Yessi.

"We can't see the real sky anymore," the shaman said. "Now the earth has a new sky. The earth has a new sun and a new moon. We live the same as animals. The grandfather sends messengers, animal spirits who warn us of danger and show us our path, but we must be watchful for them."

The shaman had silver hair streaked with black that hung to his waist. And he had deep, ebony eyes. He was frail and bent, but he was the most powerful man I knew. He spoke to the animal spirits and interpreted their messages. He had vast knowledge of the value of plants for healing. He understood their use as a gateway from the natural world to the spirit world. That knowledge gave him his importance.

"One being wanted to be master of all the earth's creatures. He haunted the jungle, enticing the souls of both the living and the dead with an eerie whistling sound. The kenaimas is hairy and knobby kneed, half man and half wolf with red eyes and teeth as sharp as knifes."

The shaman raised his fingers like talons to Aya as if he was a fighting bird and she looked frightened, but then he laughed. She giggled in return.

The most mystical of creatures were the birds that flew high over the canopy of the trees. Birds were the guardians of the place before existence. They were not bound by space or time. Birds carried messages from the grandfather to humans.

"All creatures are what they are," the shaman said, "based on their nature. None have dominion over another and each has a purpose. Animal spirits are our allies. They warn of danger, for each creature has adversaries. Animal spirits guide our journey."

My mother's spirit guide was the yellow bird. Many people in the tribe listened to her. She served bread first to the carved zemi and then to the cacique and then to the shaman before serving all the people.

"The dark man is not eternal. He'll die when we respect all creatures on the earth," the shaman concluded.

"The traders have an iron pot big enough to hold food for the whole tribe," my mother explained to the shaman.

"We must trade so the children do not wake with pains

of hunger," they all said.

"A big pot does not make food," the shaman said.

"We saw only three men," my uncle said to the cacique. "We have many more warriors."

"The Carib shaman has sent them to us by an evil spell," our shaman said. He picked up a bit of bark and handed it to Father.

Father held it over the fire until it dripped sap. He followed the interest in my eyes. "The plant's own spirit will tell me how to prepare it," he said.

Only the shaman or his apprentice may mix the leaves, prepare the infusion, and brew the potion to the best result. Prepared correctly, the brew will open the shaman's mind to truth and meaning.

The shaman drank and they all waited for him to speak.

"How does it feel?" I whispered to my father.

To my surprise, he answered me. "Warmness comes and the top of my head throbs." He patted his crown. "Vision blurs and dizziness takes me. But then I am overwhelmed by a sense of belonging. I am one with all. A great peace settles over me and the visions come."

The ancient shaman swayed in his trance.

"The kenaimas stalks the people of our village." The shaman sat in silence for a moment. "Our adversary wears many clothes: shirt, pants, boots, and a hat. What does he hide?"

The shaman handed the drink to my father who took a sip.

Mother tightly clutched in one fist the carved zemi in the center of the feather necklace she always wore.

We waited.

"Tituba morphs from a jaguar into a cricket," Father said, "and runs into an empty corner. Tituba stays very still and does not rub her legs. She hides behind the iron pot so the kenaimas cannot find her."

"What does it mean?" I asked. I had never before been called out in the visions.

One of the other women spoke. "Iron pot offers protection."

"No," the shaman said sharply. "Tituba must not hide behind the iron pot. Tituba is born to be different, but she tries to be the same. She is a flower with each petal special and unique. She is not meant to be a speck of color on the savanna."

"The trader has a knife, sharp. It cut a twig in half in one stroke." My uncle did not need to say that he wanted to have the knife. "They want baskets and shells, not our food supply."

"Tituba must be strong and brave like her spirit animal, the jaguar."

The cacique nodded his head sorrowfully. He rubbed his jaw. "Dangerous men have invaded our homeland with terrifying weapons and man-eating dogs." Only a few of the tribe had had dealings with the white men, the cacique and the shaman among them. "They chase us sitting abreast enormous beasts that respond to their will. And when caught, they force us to dig inside the ground and pull out rocks. If we had not fled and hid, we would work until we died of sickness or starvation." He paused to ensure that he had their full attention. "You can see that an evil spirit has sucked all the color from their skins leaving them as pale as death."

"The knife is useful and can help us hunt. The iron pot is good and can help us cook," my uncle said.

"The iron pot does not offer protection. The sharp edge of the knife is two-sided."

"What do you think?" the shaman asked my father and

Uncle shook his head in agreement. The shaman did this often by way of preparation of my father for his future duties.

My uncle looked to Father. He did not want a shaman. He wanted a supporter.

Father swayed. He sat in silence for a long time. He looked at Mother, me, Yessi and Aya, each of us in our turn. "The tribe is half the size it was a year ago. We must protect the women. If we risk the baby-makers, there will be no tribe soon enough."

The cacique stood and placed his hands on his hips. He looked strong, massive as a mountain. "We have no need of the white man's property. The price is too high." And so it was decided that we would not go.

But I wanted scissors. Uncle wanted a knife. Mother wanted a large cooking pot. We did not want to want these things, but wanting them bothered our thinking in the day and our dreams at night. We talked together in hushed tones of the things we wanted.

"If I dream of the knife, doesn't that mean I should have the knife?" Uncle asked. "Maybe if we meet them by accident as did the warriors and just traded for a few, small things."

"Where do you go?" asked my father when he saw me rushing to meet the others.

"I think I found a mango tree," I lied, "ripe and full of bees. Maybe honey too." Mango was one of my father's favorites. I kept quiet about my true purpose. It was the only time in my life I had lied to my father. I ran off before he could see my face flush red.

It was hottest summer and the days were long. There were ten mothers with their children who walked into the jungle to meet the traders, even though the shaman warned against it, even though the cacique forbid it. We carried our best baskets, blankets, and gourds. My uncle and three other warriors also came.

We walked until the sun was high overhead and then sheltered in a cave while a sudden thunderstorm soaked the earth. We gathered plants and wood for the fire and left them in the cave to retrieve on the way home.

After the rain, we crossed the savanna. Soon, the Orinoco flowed like a silver snake before us. We stopped and drank water and gathered green bananas from the trees. We gathered nuts to store in a clay and stick hut at the tree line that we had built for use on our travels.

We stood together on the shore, near where we hid our dugout canoes. My uncle and the other warriors took two of the canoes and went to fish. They prepared a long line that they would attach to a remora's tail. This fish had suction cups on the back of its head. The remora would attach itself to a fish and the fisherman would gently pull both into the canoe. The men gathered their line and pushed off in the canoes.

So the warriors weren't with us when a ship came into view and stopped midstream. A Carib warrior stood next to a pale-faced sailor with hair the color of sunset. Another sailor threw a heavy weight into the water and the ship stood still in the current. There were many more sailors than we had seen the day before.

The warrior smiled and waved to us, beckoned us to come to the ship. "Let's trade," the Carib warrior yelled. "We see you have gourds for water and banana."

We looked at our full baskets, but remained reluctant.

"The fruit will soon rot on the trees if you don't gather it for us." He held up fabrics in bright colors, beads that reflected the light back into our faces and then the big iron pot.

"I'm getting it," my aunt said as she loaded a basket into

a canoe. My mother looked alarmed as if my aunt stole the iron pot from her.

I knew we should wait for the men to return, but I wanted scissors.

"We've traded all up and down the river," the warrior said in a comforting voice. "No troubles."

I joined my aunt. I stepped into a canoe and lifted the oars.

We knew it was unwise to all go at once, but we were too excited. We paddled several canoes out to the ship. The captain welcomed us on board. He took our baskets and stacked them on the deck.

The captain reached out and circled his fingers around my mother's arm, I think because she was the prettiest of us. She tried to pull away, but could not. Other sailors rushed on deck and grabbed more of us. One wrapped his arm around my waist. I kicked until I twisted my way loose.

We lived on the water, so even the youngest of us could swim. We knew what we were supposed to do. We were to jump into the river, swim to shore, and then run to the village. I pushed Yessi into the water. I picked up Aya and tossed her in the same direction. Yessi floated for a few moments in the current and than circled her arms around Aya and took strong strokes toward the shore.

Mother screamed at me to jump, but I couldn't leave her. I twisted the skin on the captain's arm and kicked his ankles until he yelped and let her go.

Mother and I dove together into the river, but the captain grabbed my foot at the last minute. I slammed against the wooden side of the boat and blood poured from my nose. I couldn't breathe. The captain pulled me back into the ship. He held my arms tight. I struggled but couldn't pull loose.

I was tied with thick ropes. The others who had escaped

into the water were swimming under the surface with all the grace and strength of the pink dolphin. Yessi swam out and helped each one to the shore.

The captain ordered his sailors to paddle our canoes out to catch the runaways. The sailors jumped into the boats, paddling with their thick arms to easily overtake the women who remained in the water. They pulled them inside the canoes and held tight even as the women screamed and squirmed.

My mother swam along the side of the ship in the opposite direction from the shore. When the canoes were far enough away, she climbed a line up the hull of the boat. She came for me, but my bounds were too tight.

She struggled with the ropes until the captain saw her and attacked her. Arms grabbed, flailed. I watched as the captain pulled my mother's necklace from her and it fell to the deck.

The captain swung an oar and split my mother's skull. Her blood spread across the deck toward me. I couldn't hold back the ugly sound in the back of my throat. I screamed as they threw her lifeless body into the river for the crocodiles to eat.

My eyes scanned the shoreline. Yessi stood under the protection of the lupuna trees. The trees were massive and could curse the evil spirits. Yessi handed Aya to the nearest woman and shooed the rest of other women on their journey back toward the village, but she did not want to leave without us.

She rushed toward the water to save our mother. She swam to her, dragged her to shore, rocked her body in her arms. Blood covered Yessi's arms and face. She wailed. Our mother was gone to the sky place and nothing could be done.

Yessi swam out into the river. She was coming to me until I shook my head "no." I wanted Yessi to save herself and

Aya. I wanted to tell her I was gone from her now. I wanted to tell her good-bye and wish her a good life. I wanted to tell her how much I loved her.

From the shallows, Yessi raised her hands to me and I knew she wanted to tell me these things too. She turned and ran into the growth.

On the ship's deck, I saw my mother's necklace. I thought I could reach it. I extended my fingers, touched, and then grasped it.

2
Thompson Plantation, Barbados, September 1674

My ship had been offshore for three days. After many days at sea, the sailors had opened the top hatch and did not shut it. Fresh air swirled into the hold where we were kept. The breeze held a fragrance of plants and fertile earth. The smell taunted me with scents of land, but the ship did not move beyond a gentle rocking on the waves off the shore.

I stood under the opening of the hatch and watched the seabirds floating in an azure sky, those magical messengers from the grandfather. They squawked and shrieked. I pondered what these gulls told me of my future life, but I could not make out their meaning. There were a great many of them, each screeching a high shrill sound, one on top of the other, obscuring their meaning.

The sailors lowered a bucket of water to drink and food—bananas and fish cooked with mango—into the hold. They brought more water and soap with which to wash. They lowered to us an oil that smelled of hibiscus flowers for softening our dry skin.

Soon enough, the ship sailed toward the shore. Sailors yelled as they moved heavy ropes thick as the cables in the trees. Through the open hatch, I could hear wild flipping sounds and the side of the ship pounded against something, soon discovered to be the dock.

As I stepped off the ship, I was made to stand in a fenced ring near the dock before a group of colorless men. My gaze fell to a young warrior unloading a nearby ship. He was a beautiful young man. He was brown as a cocoa bean and his shiny black hair hung over his high forehead. He was tall compared to the men of my tribe and deeply muscled from work. His eyes were narrow, nearly disappearing when he squinted into the sun.

He saw me and there was hope, desire, and recognition in his gaze. He watched me for many minutes before he strolled casually into the ring. He seemed confident and strong, but I could see pain behind his proud expression.

He looked only at me as he walked through our lot of shaking and numb women. I felt the power of his stare. It pulled me toward him. He took my hand and held it with both of his. Energy passed between us. He looked deeply into my eyes and drew me in. He stood with me as if I was his and I began to feel as if I was.

A young wispy man of an age not many more years than my own spoke to the warrior in a language I did not understand. He, too, had hurt in his eyes, his pain so strong it seemed as if it was difficult for him to live.

The handsome warrior responded to the fragile man's question in a way that made the man's lips curl up. He pointed to me.

The pale man had made an assumption. The warrior turned to me, pleading silently, near panic. I didn't understand the words, but I knew that I was making a choice for or against this handsome man. I smiled into my shoulder and said nothing.

The warrior said in a tribal tongue not too far removed from my own, "Please speak your name to this man."

"Tituba," I said.

And so it appeared to the gaunt man that we were one. He spoke for a long time with a man who held a leather book. Their voices rose and fell as if on the cusp of an argument, but they never appeared to become truly angry.

The warrior held my hand tightly as we watched. His hand was large, strong, with many calluses. His fingers touching mine made me feel less alone.

On the ship, I had felt weak, lightheaded. I couldn't control the wings that fluttered in my chest. Breath had often come too fast with no air making it inside. But when the handsome man held my hand in his big one, I felt protected. I felt hope.

I also felt aware for the first time in days. I understood that I had left my previous life behind and this was my new life. I understood that this man was the bridge that I needed to help me pass over to that new life.

Soon enough we were both shuffled onto a cart.

"John," he whispered into my ear as we settled in and I knew that was his name.

John was tense until we were well down the road and the town had faded from existence, but soon after that his eyelids grew heavy. We both allowed the rocking of the cart to lull us into a fitful sleep.

In a short time, I woke to the fire in John's hand. His face was flushed and wet. He was sick or injured in some way that I could not see with my eyes. His body was heated from the inside to fight off the malevolent spirits that invaded. Chained to the cart, there was little I could do besides hold him upright and whisper calming words.

It was two days later when the cart arrived at the Thompson Plantation. We came at night and were shoved into a wattle and daub hut with a thatched roof. This was the home of a strange dark-skinned family who could not speak to us, but addressed each other with words we did not comprehend. The family vacated the hut to let us have some privacy.

When John and I were alone, he lifted off his shirt. I

saw the raw lash marks across his back, a thick layer of blood-matted gashes over old scars. I wondered how he could have even stood upright with such pain. The dark woman returned carrying a bowl of water and some clean cloth. I cleaned his wounds and wished I had more to offer.

The next morning, we were sent to work in the fields. As we shuffled toward the cane, I saw the pale man with his sickness of the body. I stopped him with my hand and the foreman raised his whip. John shoved me behind him in a protective stance.

"It's fine," Mr. Thompson must have said because the foreman lowered his whip. Mr. Thompson looked in my eyes. I imagined that he said, "What do you wish to say, girl?"

I asked John to tell him that if I had the right herbs, I could make an easing tea for his suffering.

He was taken aback, but paused in reflection. "I have a very fine physician," he told John and John made the meaning clear to me.

I waited, unable to further my case without the words.

After our day in the fields, Mr. Thompson, for that was his name, appeared. He walked with John and I through his gardens and the nearby wood. His mother, Mrs. Pearsehouse, joined us. She walked warily behind us watching my every move.

I found a fire bush, bright with red flowers. I picked the green leaves tinted red on the borders.

"The leaves from the fire bush help to ease pain," I said. "Tell him that a vine called cat's claw would be better though," I told John.

Under Mrs. Pearsehouse's watchful eye, I made Mr. Thompson a tea of the several plants I'd found for pain, fever, and swelling. Mrs. Pearsehouse watched as I mashed the plants with what I came to know as a mortar and pestle and added bark to simmering hot water in the fireplace of the kitchen. When it had steeped long enough, she indicated to me that I should take an experimental sip and then she waited a few minutes.

She allowed me to take the pot of tea to her son, but she poured it out into delicate little cups with a pattern of flowers on them. At the time, I had never seen such a thing.

He sat under the cover of a roof outside in the cool evening breeze. He wished to appear at ease, but the tightness around his mouth and the hooding of his eyes belied this. He sipped the tea. It calmed his face as he relaxed.

Mrs. Pearsehouse patted her son's thin hand. She stayed by his side while I returned to the kitchen.

I siphoned off the dregs of the tea to take to John. I also made an infusion with water, aloe, and fish oil for John. I soaked the leaves until they were soft and later that night, laid the leaves across his back. John reacted to my efforts by relaxing, similar to Mr. Thompson's response.

As a result of the tea I'd made for Mr. Thompson, I was made a house slave to cook and care for the young master and his mother. A large African woman with a years-old burn on her right cheek spent many days teaching me the rudiments for making the bland and sugary food the English liked. She also showed me how to prepare the foods of her people that ignited the tongue so that the eyes made a waterfall to put it out.

And much work needed to be done in the garden to make it sufficient for treating the master. The African cook seemed happy to have me go outside and dig in the dirt, making it ready for the plants I thought we would need.

For many nights, I watched John sleep. He was riddled with pain after the exertion of his day's work. He removed his shirt and I covered his back with the infusion. Sometimes it took many minutes before his eyelids grew heavy and he drifted off. Sometimes he could not hold them open for brief seconds after he lay down.

I memorized all the details of his back. I loved the spread of his muscles across its width, ending in a pronounced arrow shape at each shoulder. I loved how his back narrowed at the waist like a pathway to the roundness of his backside. I watched as the lash marks on his back healed over time leaving angry red lines that made a pattern like bark on a tree. In its own way, it was beautiful.

I was conscious of my own attraction to John, but also fearful of what might occur once he found his full health. I was still just a girl. Too young. Afraid. Still, I could not resist the impulse to touch his silken, ebony hair. He moaned and half turned toward me.

But I had no cause for concern. Once John was strong and well, he never touched me beyond holding my hand. My hand—this he had difficulty letting go. He held it at every opportunity.

He worked in the fields from sunrise to sunset and then helped me to overturn the soil in the garden and put in plants that I suggested. He completed any task asked of him without complaint. And then, for several hours each evening, he and a few of the African men endeavored to build us our own hut. He was an attentive student as the African slaves taught him. Before long, we were able to move into our private corner of the plantation, within sight of the main house, on the garden side of the slave compound.

I weaved mats and baskets from the grasses that grew along the bay. I filled the baskets with fruits from the trees. I emptied and dried gourds that I filled with water. Most evenings John caught a fish for us.

John quickly learned the nuances of my language and taught me some of the words used on the plantation.

"It's called English. It must be spoken properly," he said, "or they get angry."

Mrs. Pearsehouse allowed me to practice speaking my English with her. She taught me how to serve high tea, how to use a spinning wheel, how to survive as a slave.

John and I relaxed. Mrs. Pearsehouse was kind. The master was appreciative. There was always plenty of food in the sea, the garden or in the trees. We ate, even if it was just what remained on a serving tray.

And we talked.

In the quiet of one night, John told me that he had been on the island of Barbados for about two years when he found me. He was from the valley of the Orinico River same as me, but he was from a different tribe. He had been captured, enslaved and purchased by a sugar cane farmer.

"He was a cruel man. I would have done anything to leave him behind," John explained. "The farmer's property was small and remote, but he had visions of a great plantation and so he worked us day and night, until sickness and death took all but three of us."

"So it could be worse," I said.

"Yes. Much worse."

I took his hand as he had done so many times before. John kept his eyes on our entwined fingers.

"I was unloading a crate of supplies from a ship in the harbor when I saw a group of slave women enter the ring."

"The farmer?" I asked, knowing that there was always someone watching.

"He had disappeared the night before with a lady in a frilly dress. He had not visited town in some time." John touched my hair and ran a finger along the line of my jaw. "I had not seen a native woman myself in two years."

"So then what?" I asked.

The farmer had hired a sort of overseer for the night. The farmer had me open a crate filled with bottles of rum. The farmer took two and wondered off. The overseer drank from a third as we finished unloading the supplies from the ship. By the time we were nearly finished, the overseer had become quite drunk.

"I didn't think about it," John continued. "I didn't make a plan or consider the possible consequences. I walked away from that life into the slave ring and selected the woman I wanted. You."

That made John a runaway. "But?" I couldn't formulate a clear question.

I want a son," he told me. He noted the look of distress in my eyes. "Or a pretty little girl like you will make me proud as well," he said.

I did not mention at that time that I didn't want to bring a baby, a little boy or girl, into this life. I still reeled from the loss of my sisters. I knew they were in the world. I knew they needed me, wanted me, and there was nothing I could do to get back to them. A tear clouded my eye. I lay my forehead on John's chest so he wouldn't see.

"I'm not sure how I was sold to Mr. Thompson" John said. "Maybe Mr. Thompson made a deal with the farmer. More likely, the harbormaster sold me again with little thought to who I was or where I had come from. Whatever, it can't be a bad thing to put as many miles as possible between me and that little farm."

In that moment, I wanted nothing more than to be connected to his man, to be bound in love to him. I touched my lips to his.

"You know I would never ask you to do something you did not wish to do," he said.

"I know." I kissed him again.

3
Thompson Plantation, Barbados, December 1679

I lifted my face to the Caribbean sun and reveled in its warmth. The calm blue of the sky mixed with the last streaks of strong orange that marked the rising of the day.

I tossed my cap and let down my long black hair. The air was balmy, heavy with the weight of water, but it wasn't as sizzling as it would be later in the day. I lifted the weight of my hair for a moment to feel the breeze on the back of my damp neck.

I ran like my spirit animal, the jaguar, through lush, floral vegetation, my skin glowing copper in the heat. Blue and green parrots sang in the trees overhead as a gecko slithered across my path. The aromas of peat and blossoms filled my nostrils with their sweetness. As I ran, I flung away my smock.

I approached the bay, kicked off my shoes and stripped to my petticoat. A simple seed and feather necklace that had been covered by my European clothes decorated my shoulders. Without a pause, I dived into the deep blue water and came up mid-bay into John's wet arms. He kissed me on the lips, down my neck and across my shoulder.

John showed me his uniform teeth, white as a clamshell, as he carried me dripping out of the water and lay down beside me on a blanket of green. He peeled and fed me a banana as he feasted on my neck. He rubbed my stomach with the palm of his hand.

"I want to fill you with babies," he said, not for the first time.

I slid his hand away from me. I had told him the truth. I did not want our love to be based on a lie. I'd told him that I did not wish to have children, but he chose to ignore that.

"You love children," John whispered. "You would love our child most of all."

"You know how I feel about it." My heart raced as desire swam through me. I let John believe he had won this particular disagreement. He did fill me and I wished for it. He knew that I knew herbs and methods to deter pregnancy. I knew that he felt less of a man as the years passed by with no children between us.

I would love my child. I would do anything for my child. But, my child would not be my own. I promised myself I would never bear slave children.

After my swim with John, I approached the main house. The mansion was white with tall columns. A porch wrapped the outside. Mostly African slaves worked in and around it, but the master rarely saw the difference between the Africans and Indians. We understood the difference and even as we learned to live together.

A young African girl handed me a basket of fruit she had picked. This little one was as sweet as her fruit. She helped me to explain my time missing from the house. I lifted the basket and rested it on the top of my head. I patted her cheek in thanks.

As I stepped into the foyer, I saw the master's mother, Mrs. Pearsehouse, rushing around instructing the house slaves. She carried an armful of bright, tropical flowers that she set on a table near a waiting crystal vase.

By European standards, the bodice of Mrs. Pearsehouse's dress was a bit too low and the color a bit too bright for this time in the morning, but I liked her brightness. I thought her spirit animal must be a macaw—colorful, free, but with a dangerous beak if provoked.

"There you are Tituba. Really, these morning baths of yours are getting way too long." Mrs. Pearsehouse appraised my appearance. "And you've lost your cap again, haven't you?" She touched the ends of my loose hair. "Hurry. There is much to do today before the party."

I pushed my limits as far as they would go. She didn't like that, but she wasn't really angry. I could tell. I couldn't help a quiet smile and looked down to hide it lest I rile her. "Yes, Ma'am."

Mrs. Pearsehouse pulled the basket of fruit from my arms and examined it. "Help with the cooking today. Make that molasses cake I like so well and do something with all this fruit."

"Yes Ma'am."

Mrs. Pearsehouse shook her head in mock annoyance. "Goodness," she said. She picked up a long stem topped with an orange hibiscus bloom from the table and began a floral arrangement.

"And go and find your cap."

Guests arrived by carriage for the party. They traveled a path lined by palms and fire torches. The house was bright with the shine of candles and alive with activity.

The doors and windows were all flung open to let in a chill evening breeze. On a table in the foyer, an enormous arrangement of red anthurium, blue ginger, orange hibiscus, and white orchids greeted the guests.

I walked through the party, greeting guests with a serving platter of food. Each guest held a glass of rum or wine and the laughter had already grown too loud. I weaved my way through groups in conversation and couples dancing.

Mr. Samuel Parris gave off a stormy countenance as he stepped into the foyer. His visage was altogether disquieting and his composure was as stiff as the new suit he wore. He was altogether incongruent with the party atmosphere. I approached, as I knew I must, and bowed.

He lifted a tart made from mangos and cane sugar from my silver tray and took a small bite. His face relaxed and I was rewarded with a slight lifting of his lips. "This is delicious," he said. "Did you make it?"

I nodded yes, quietly pleased with his compliment. I felt the blush that spread from my neck to my face as I moved through the crowd. I could feel his eyes follow me. There was something animal, predatory in his manner, as if he stalked me.

Mr. Thompson, sickly and especially weak despite his young age, sat on a sofa. I stayed close by in case he was in need of help, only occasionally moving through the room to refill a beverage or make a round with the tray.

Mr. Parris joined him. Mr. Thompson and Mr. Parris were both young men, both thin and fair, yet Mr. Thompson was like a withering twig fallen from a tall tree and Mr. Parris was like the tree's looming shadow.

"The Indians of Venezuela and Guiana are a peaceful people, usually more calm than the Africans," Mr. Thompson said. "Family people with a great fondness for children. Good cooks too."

Mr. Parris's eyes roamed the room and then came to linger on me. He twisted his neck to bring me into full view. Mr. Parris's hair was wispy at the top. It was the color of dried straw. He attempted to make up for it with a bit of a flourish of hair under his upper lip. His skin was ruddy - likely from sun exposure - in a way that contributed to his unhappy look.

I backed toward the long wall opposite the dancers. I wished people would cross in front of me and obstruct his view.

"Yes," Mr. Thompson said. "Excellent choice, but she is important to me. She cares for my health."

Mr. Parris gave Mr. Thomas a long and appraising look.

Mrs. Pearsehouse joined the gentlemen. Mr. Parris stood and offered her his seat.

"This is my mother, Mrs. Elizabeth Pearsehouse," Mr. Thompson said. He nodded to the gentlemen with him. "Mr. Samuel Parris."

Mr. Parris nodded. After Mrs. Pearsehouse had situated herself comfortably, he pulled over a wooden chair.

"May I offer my condolences on the passing of your father?" Mrs. Pearsehouse said to Mr. Parris. "I had met him on numerous occasions."

"Kind of you to say."

"My son says that you left your studies at Harvard to come to Barbados to take up your inheritance."

"Yes."

"And how long have you been on the island?" Mrs. Pearsehouse asked.

"Close to five years now. I so wished to join my name to those of you who are plantation owners here in Barbados, but my father's plantation suffered too severely in the hurricane. It hasn't fully recovered," Mr. Parris said.

"With time and effort, the plantation can be restored," Mrs. Pearsehouse noted. "It's a wonderful prospect. I visited there a few times. It was delightful."

It was as clear to me as it was to Mrs. Pearsehouse that her pointed questions were unwelcome to Mr. Parris.

"Mother," Mr. Thompson interjected, "the 1675 hurricane was a most devastating and cruel storm. No need to ask if the plantation faired well. Not much of the west coast survived."

I had heard of this storm. Hundred of people were killed. Homes, crops, and livestock were destroyed. The west coast was laid to waste.

"As luck would have it," Mr. Parris said, "I had already situated myself in Bridgetown."

"Oh."

"Mr. Parris was acting as a credit agent for the sugar farmers."

"But no more?" Mrs. Pearsehouse asked. "What are your plans now?"

"Mr. Parris is in a hurry to sell the estate and conclude his late father's affairs so that he may return to Boston," Mr. Thompson told his mother.

"And what hurries you to Boston, Mr. Parris?"

"I have an Elizabeth of my own in that town and we are anxious to marry and start a family," Mr. Parris said.

"Congratulations, sir," Mrs. Pearsehouse replied. "I can understand your rush."

"And what employ do you plan to undertake there?" Mr. Thompson asked.

"At the first, I plan to rent a mercantile," Mr. Parris responded, "and bring the bounty of the islands to New England."

"A mercantile. How interesting? But, no land? Your father was a landholder in England, was he not?"

"A modest landowner," Mr. Parris said.

I moved away from their conversation with my silver tray, but Mr. Parris's eyes clung to me wherever I stepped in the room. I wished he would let loose his hold on me.

Mr. Thompson watched this. He let out a resolved exhalation and said, "I believe that Mr. Parris and I have settled a delicate matter."

Mr. Parris nodded his agreement. They shook hands.

"Mr. Parris will take Tituba for his household in order to settle our debt with his father."

Mrs. Pearsehouse looked stunned. "No. Surely another will do."

"No," Mr. Parris said.

I gripped my chest and was overcome by a deep feeling of helplessness. I couldn't breathe. My heart pounded. My hands went numb and my skin took on a cold clamminess.

I ran out, even before the last of the guests had left. I escaped through the door and ran across the lawn. I found John outside our thatch hut. He played a ceremonial drum alongside two African men. His naked chest glistened with perspiration and his arms were solid with effort. The Africans had also removed their shirts and coats. Other slaves drank as they danced around the fire.

The shaman chewed on a few leaves and soon began to sway in a trance. This shaman was young and fierce, his face painted with white lines, and he wore an intricate woven headpiece. The shaman was neither Indian nor African. He was from an island called Ayti. I had heard some of the whites call this island Haiti, the place of the Taino. He was the only holy man John and I had to guide us. We liked him. We trusted him.

I moved near to the fire, chanting along with the shaman to help to control my breathing. I let my hair loose and stripped to my cotton shift.

John saw my distress. He stood and mopped his chest with his shirt before he put it on. He came to me, wrapped his arm around my neck and pulled me into his chest.

I sobbed into him as I struggled to keep my emotions in check. I choked out one word: "sold."

The shaman rested his hands on my shoulders as he examined the agony in my eyes. He painted my face an angry red. He held up two pieces of cloth and then tied the cloth into knots resembling a doll. The shaman handed the doll to me. I raised the doll toward the fire.

A demon stepped from the shadows on the opposite side of the fire. For a moment, it looked as if he walked through the fire, a tall, dark figure in black clothes. His face was contorted into a look of pure rage. Black evil. I held my hands over my mouth to stifle my scream. Only a peep of terror escaped my lips.

Mr. Parris yelled. "Conjurer!" He smacked me across the face. He pulled the doll from my hands and tossed it to the ground and stomped it. "There will be none of this in my household." He stomped away, back into the shadows.

Every face in the circle looked at the doll on the ground. With the exception of John, each one was a portrait of horror. John's face showed his pure, red rage. The shaman let out a primal shriek that chilled the blood. He flung his arms to the night sky to cast away predatory spirits.

The sun was bright when Mr. Parris stepped through the front entry the next morning. He nodded to Mrs. Pearsehouse.

"Thank you for coming." Mrs. Pearsehouse waved him into the morning parlor.

I caught a glimpse of a guest and followed behind my mistress. I was on my best behavior, trying to make myself as useful as could be. It was my intent to ask if they wanted refreshment, but then I heard my name. I stood just around the corner and listened to their private conversation.

"There is a matter I wish to discuss with you," Mrs. Pearsehouse said. "Tituba is married."

"Before God?" Mr. Parris asked.

"No. Well, I don't know. It was from before. I'm sure they had some sort of tribal thing. Maybe a church, maybe not, uh, but they were married just the same. We don't break up families on this plantation."

Mr. Parris made no mention of the events of the previous evening. In the night, I'd allowed myself to hope that he would be so put off as to change his mind. It was an unlikely prospect as most of the slaves practice similar rituals and he would know that.

"What is his name? This husband."

"He refuses to reveal his proper name. They say he thinks his identity will be lost. We call him John. John Indian."

"I have no use for a buck," Mr. Parris said.

"He's young, strong. He works well in the house or out in the fields."

Mr. Parris looked unconvinced.

"What will your Elizabeth think of your returning to Boston with a beautiful, young woman in tow, even if she is a slave woman? Won't she be happier if Tituba is legally married with a man of her own?"

"I see your point." He considered. "Of course, I had not planned to make such a purchase. How much do you care to keep the two together?"

I listened to silence for an unbearable period of time.

"Half price," she finally responded.

"We'll have the words said again before God." He glanced over toward where I stood as if he saw me through the wall. "And she will act the good Christian woman at all times. He was striking a bargain with me—for John. Forget all that I am and I may have John with me.

"Then you'll take them both?" Mrs. Pearsehouse smiled in satisfaction until she caught a glimpse of me out the corner of her eye.

John tended the red potato plants in the garden. He

stopped when he saw me running toward him. He stretched his back and squinted into the morning sun to watch me.

Mrs. Pearsehouse followed me into the garden. "I'm sorry. I planned to speak to you later today, after we settled a few things."

I stared at her.

"Mr. Parris agreed to take you both. That's the best I can do for you, Tituba."

"Across the island? To his plantation?" John asked, a bit of fear in his tone at the prospect of being so close to his previous owner.

"On the sea," Mrs. Pearsehouse answered.

John looked across the vista toward an expanse of unending blue. He didn't know what that meant. Neither did I. He clenched his jaw and worked to settle his face.

John and I had laid in the dark through the long night and imagined that we had options. John had heard of a cave where we might hide until we could construct a raft of bamboo timbers sturdy enough to float us toward our homeland. I pictured myself gathering mangos and bananas for the trip. We both instinctively understood that this would be our last chance to go home.

In the morning, Mrs. Pearsehouse appraised the anxious look in my eyes and John's restless, seething anger. She read his face as well as I could. "Have you seen that cage for runaway slaves in the market square?"

I jumped back. *I can't live in a cage*, I thought. My breathing quickened and my heart pounded at just the mention of it.

John didn't know what to do with his anger. He was not a slave, but a free man in waiting. He wanted to go home. He would find it hard to give up that dream.

He called me a dead leaf butterfly. Like that butterfly, I changed appearance to be whoever I needed to be to survive in the world I lived in. I wore the custom, learned to speak the words, and acted as I was told. He couldn't do that, so he stayed silent and waited his chance. This did not appear to be it.

Mrs. Pearsehouse beckoned to me to follow her and I did. We returned to the big house and went into Mrs. Pearsehouse's bedroom.

"I'm not sure I want John to come with me," I said. I couldn't save myself, but I maybe could save John.

"Nonsense," Mrs. Pearsehouse said. She opened a large trunk and pulled out a dark woolen dress and a heavy, rich, deep, but bright blue shawl the color of an ocean orchid. Mrs. Pearsehouse called it royal blue. "Here. You'll need these much more than I do."

"He doesn't want to come." I looked at the heavy garments with reluctance.

"Of course he does. He loves you." Mrs. Pearsehouse touched my arm. "I'm not saying that it won't be different. It will, but you'll be fine. What makes you so afraid?"

"I have the most overwhelming feeling of dread."

"People in Massachusetts are like me, some maybe a little better, some a little worse. They're just people." She smiled.

I tried a weak smile in return.

Yellow canaries perched in the trees. Flowers bloomed around the garden path. A heavy, sweet aroma filled the air. The family sat in the gazebo, warmed from the afternoon sun. Mr. Thompson covered his legs with a blanket.

A few of the plantation slaves, many of them children, bordered the fence at the garden's edge. A handful of other slaves stopped their work and looked on from the fields.

I wore a cream-colored dress, a discard of Mrs. Pearsehouse. My hair was loose, the way that John preferred it. A tiny yellow canary swooped in front of me as I walked down the garden path and stood beside John.

John was scrubbed clean and he wore a new shirt he got from I know not where. His eyes locked with mine as I moved toward him. He smiled as he twined a garland of buds into my hair - white the color of wholeness and new beginnings.

Mr. Parris stomped into the garden. "Where's your cap?" He pulled the flowers from my hair. "We'll not proceed until she's dressed properly. This is no papist ceremony."

Mrs. Pearsehouse sent a girl for my cap. The four of us stood in awkward silence.

"She's always losing her..." Mr. Parris's scowl was so final, Mrs. Pearsehouse didn't go on.

I watched John as he stamped down his feelings. He was biding his time. Later, his eyes said. Our time is later.

Shortly, the girl returned. I pinned up my hair and covered it with the cap. At the last minute, I pushed the stems of a few of the white flowers behind my ear under my coif.

An Englishman began speaking. I had lived on the Thompson Plantation for six years. I understood almost all the words said to me. "Dearly beloved…" he went on. Then he said, "what God has joined together, let no man put asunder…"

"Skip that part," Mr. Parris bellowed. "We don't say that for slaves."

John and I went through the motions of this unfamiliar ceremony. We did what we were told. We said what we were told. I was happy that whatever my fate held, John would be with me. John was unhappy that his fate was not his own to determine.

Outside our hut that night, the Africans drummed and danced at a furious pace. Inside the hut, I huddled with John on a mat on the floor. It was hot, but I shivered uncontrollably. John rubbed my arms and whispered little noises into my ear.

I clutched a three-pointed stone with sharp edges carved with an elaborate design. One side of the stone had an impression of a god's head with the opposite side showing hunched legs. Through the middle of the stone was a hole. It's a special token of the Zemi for protection. It was given by the shaman of my tribe to my mother. It was not from the Africans or the Taino shaman.

"It's to take and keep with you always," the shaman had told my mother. He untied her seed and feather necklace and added the stone as a centerpiece.

John pulled me close to him and we both cupped our hands around my necklace.

"When you feel afraid, I want you to hold this necklace," the shaman had said to my mother, "and the Zemi will protect you."

Morning came too soon. Mr. Parris climbed aboard a wagon where John and I sat chained in the back. Mrs. Pearsehouse stepped out the front door onto the porch of the main house. She waved as we drove away.

For two days, we rode by tall, gabled houses mixed with squat huts, the land divided into parcels. On my side, the beach barely held back the jungle. On John's side, tracks of land planted with sugar cane interrupted the tangle of rainforest. Men and women with anguished or dulled faces worked the cane. Children who were barely able carried buckets of water. Overseers with whips or guns lined the fields. John couldn't pull his eyes from this view. His leg twitched and he held my hand too tightly. Maybe it was best that we left the proximity of his nightmare.

At the port, a three-mast ship was anchored. Mr. Parris joined the harbormaster and the ship's captain on the pier. As

Mr. Parris's personal items were loaded into the ship's hold, the harbormaster marked down an inventory in a small, leather-bound journal. There were trunks and boxes. Marked down. There were sacks of sugar and barrels of molasses. Marked down. Me, John, and three other slaves, all young girls, were hustled onto the ship. The five of us, marked in the book. The harbormaster put the book into his pocket.

The booming of canons signaled our life's change. Large and small ships, of which we were just one, retreated from several wharfs. We took to the open sea. The ship cast forlorn shadows over the waves.

From the deck, the island of Barbados grew smaller. The trees that made a green canopy over vividly colored flowers slipped away. Each plantation, its own village carved into the shoreline, disappeared. The last to go was a long stretch of white sand lined with turquoise water.

We were locked into the hold of the ship. I couldn't snatch enough air for my lungs. My chest ached.

4

Atlantic Ocean, Winter 1680

I awoke in the hold of the ship. We had been sunk down into this dank, airless cave. The only source of light was a hatch that a sailor opened once per day to throw down some johnnycake. At each viewing, we saw the same vast, empty blue sky.

The hold was fairly large. It held more cargo than the five of us. It was filled with trunks, barrels, and boxes. John moved the boxes around to arrange them in such a way as to protect us from some of the cold. I stood and helped him. We ventured a look into some containers that could be breached without notice.

The first box we opened contained glasses of different sizes with the same floral pattern etched on each. One of the glasses was broken. There was a clock buried deep in straw and a pair of candlesticks that shined our reflection back to us like still water.

A second crate contained two decorative boxes. The first held a long string of pearls and other baubles. The second held cigars I had seen hang from white men's mouths. Each of these things was packed as if they were precious. Other than a few blankets and a bundle of herbs and spices, there was little of interest to me.

Food must be stored elsewhere. Other than the scant johnnycake, there was little to eat or drink, save the bugs that invaded our space.

Each day the weather grew colder. I made my way to

my trunk. From it, I put on Mrs. Pearsehouse's winter dress directly over my own light summer dress. I wrapped Mrs. Pearsehouse's blue shawl over John's shoulders. We huddled together under one of the blankets. I rested my hand on my throat and covered the spot where my necklace with the zemi figure lay against my skin.

I looked with sympathy to the three African slave girls huddled together in the damp, freezing hold. All three were strangers to John and me.

The eldest of the three, named Ealasaid, was maybe fifteen years of age. She sat stiffly with a look of bold defiance on her face. She crossed her arms and scolded everyone with her eyes. Her chin jutted out whenever I glanced at her.

The next eldest was called Lala. She was lovely with a pleasant, wide-open expression. She had black bruises, as I did, from being tossed against the side of the ship and the contents of the hold.

The smallest one, Sayen, was a girl barely twelve years old. She had been severely affected by the raging of the seas the night before. Although the morning had brought relief, she kept a chamber pot close at hand.

A creature I had never before seen bit Ealasaid. The animal was brownish-gray, about the size of John's foot with whiskers like a jungle cat. It scampered to the girl on four feet and bit her toe for no known reason. John caught it and handed it to her to eat raw. She did.

I beckoned the girls over and the two younger joined the huddle with John and me. We wrapped arms and I made the shawl go as far as it could. Eventually, Ealasaid joined us as well.

Many days passed this way. Loud noises I could not identify, along with the stomping of sailors' feet and their constant yelling, filled my days. Cold and hunger filled my nights.

The ship seemed to be slowing its pace, and then one day stopped. We heard shouting and the heavy anchor sink into the water.

The sailor left the hatch open so fresh air filled the hold. It smelled of fish and people, but under that scent was the lovely scent of green. We all stood and breathed in.

The sailor sent down a meal of fish and fresh vegetables. I recognized this pattern from my arrival in Barbados. We were being trussed for sale. I knew I should not, but, I was hungry and so I ate.

When the sailor sent down a pitcher of oil that smelled of fresh roses, I didn't want to spread the oil on my skin, but my fingers were so cracked and dry that they hardly opened, so I did.

We waited to be taken to the ring to be sold like livestock, but this did not happen. The ship grew quiet as the sailors went off leaving us behind. The sun moved lower in the sky and still we were not moved.

With the fire of sunset behind him, Mr. Parris stood over us and looked down into the hold. I had not seen him since we left Barbados. With him was another man. Each held a crystal glass of amber liquid as if attending a party.

Their conversation took on a certain cadence, the sound of an auction in progress. Mr. Parris pointed to Ealasaid and Sayen. His partner pointed to Lala and Mr. Parris shook his head. The man wanted John and Mr. Parris considered for a long time. Mr. Parris pointed to a stack of sacks that I knew contained cane. He held up one finger. His partner held up two. The two men shook hands.

Night came and still nothing happened. We heard the sailors return, singing and laughing loudly. Their sleep was accented by especially loud snores, but before the sun was up, the sailors were at their tasks.

Ealasaid and Sayen, plus two sacks of cane, were removed from the hold. The ship set sail on the early tide. Lala cried all day. I often thought it was more painful to remember those that lived and you knew that you would never again see, than to remember the ones who had died. I held her as she sobbed.

The ship slowed to a stop again. I came out of the hold blinking. Yards of sails flapped in the wind on masts that towered above me. The sails snapped and cracked like some crazy bird. This was the sound I had heard. I stumbled over snake-like coils of rope as I gingerly made my way to the wooden rail of the ship. The sun was in the morning sky, but it shined as if the great spirit had dimmed it. It had lost its vibrancy and everything I saw was gray. Gray is the color of anxiety.

5
Boston, Winter 1680

The air was colder than I knew it possible to be. It punished me with a wet, brutal wind. I was startled by bits of frozen water falling from the sky onto my face. I touched my wet cheek. I had no words for this. I had no words for much of what I saw.

We were in a cove. Several tall ships were docked in a waterfront district that shared some features with docks I had seen in Barbados. Square buildings made of wood planks or perfectly square red stones filled a savanna that lined the shore for as far as I could see. The buildings were tall and blocked all view of trees.

On the pier, Mr. Parris spoke with a different harbormaster. They divided the items in the hold. Some things went to the left toward a wagon that I presumed would go to Mr. Parris's house. Other things went right to who knew where. A trunk went left. A sack of sugar went right. Again, the harbormaster recorded it all in a book.

As the sun disappeared behind the buildings, a seaman jostled us off the ship. I was pushed left toward the wagon and Mr. Parris's household. I watched as Lala went right. She had been fed and oiled again. She was made to wear a stiff dress that crinkled when she walked. The dress was the color of coral and cut low in the bodice in a way even Mrs. Pearsehouse would call inappropriate. Plus, she wore no sleeves in the freezing air.

The harbormaster stood next to John. I held my breath.

Mr. Parris and the harbormaster talked for what seemed like an eternity. Finally, John moved left and came to stand next to me. I let out my breath and blinked back tears. John reached behind my skirts and took hold of my trembling hand.

We were instructed to climb into the back of the wagon, as Mr. Parris clicked for the horses to move.

A starry night fell over the town of Boston. Mr. Parris stopped the wagon at the door to the customhouse. He handed the reins to John. "Stay here. Don't move," he said.

He walked across the street and left us alone in this bewildering place. I stood next to John and shivered in the cold as we waited for Mr. Parris to return. I could see John thinking about how easy it would be to flick the reins on the horses and go. I laid a restraining hand on his arm.

I was too afraid of the unknown, but John was always hatching a plan for escape. I couldn't imagine a place where our situation would be better. One had but to look at his scarred back to know that John knew how much worse things could become. He'd bide his time, do what was asked of him, as long as our circumstances were reasonably fine, but he'd make a plan if one day they were not. He would never allow anyone to harm me.

Finally, Mr. Parris exited the customhouse. He stood on the street and talked to the harbormaster. The harbormaster carried his book. In a few minutes, a seaman approached. The seaman dragged Lala with him. The girl was newly cut and bruised and still woefully underdressed for the bitter cold.

A fourth man, tall, imposing, and grim, exited the customhouse and gave a few coins to Mr. Parris. The harbormaster made a notation in the journal. The seaman released his hold on Lala. The fourth man took the slave girl away. My eyes froze with tears.

In time, Mr. Parris led us into a wooden door that was part of a façade made of the strange red stones. Many houses shared this common wall, each having a door with an arched entry.

Mr. Parris looked at John. "Bring it all inside," he instructed. John and I unloaded the wagon.

Inside, the house was shared with another family who lived on the top floor. Mr. Parris's space was on the first and second floor. The first floor was small, just a few rooms, nothing like the master's big two-story house in Barbados. The parlor and kitchen were in the front. In the back was one small office.

Mr. Parris pointed this way and that directing us where to place items from the cart. John set down the last trunk. The rooms seemed overly full to me.

Mr. Parris indicated a hearth by the kitchen fire. "You sleep there. Stay on this floor unless I invite you upstairs."

John nodded, responding for us both.

"Make me something to eat before you retire for first sleep," Mr. Parris said. He handed me a sack and I opened it as Mr. Parris slipped into the back room carrying several boxes.

I unloaded foodstuff on a wooden table: orange spears with dirt on the bottom and leaves at the top that may be some kind of root; little white seeds that looked like some kind of bug larvae; and an animal loin wrapped in butcher paper. There was also a loaf of bread.

I gave John a panicked look. "I don't know this food." I held up the meat. It looked so different from the fruits and fishes of Barbados.

Mr. Parris returned with a blanket. He handed it to me.

"I don't have enough work for both of you. Starting tomorrow you'll spend your days helping out Mrs. Juliet

DuVille. She's a milliner."

I had no idea what a milliner might be.

I chopped up the animal meat and threw it into boiling water with the roots and larvae, and then watched to see what they would do. I pulled the small pouch of spices I had found on the ship from my trunk and dotted the stew with black and green specks. The meat turned gray, the roots became soft and the larvae puffed up. I put the stew and bread on the small table.

Mr. Parris gave the unpleasant appearance of the food an odd look. "It doesn't have the same appeal as your fruit tarts."

He closed his eyes and prayed for a moment and then he ate. I prayed too that this meal would be eatable. He nodded, indicating that he liked the taste well enough. He filled his bowl a second time before he allowed John and I to sit on the floor on the mats by the hearth and eat a plate. We were also curious about this new taste.

The next morning, Mr. Parris took us on the wagon. We went past many red buildings that were three or four stories tall. John heard the word brick to describe the red stones. Soon the buildings turned into widely separated houses with tall gables and colored exteriors. The trees outside were little more than tall sticks with no leaves.

There were also churches with towering spires and red doors and stores with shiny representations mounted to the wall of the products stored inside. There was a cup of ale outside a pub, an open volume outside a bookstore, a clock where they must sell clocks. We came to a store where the front window was filled with ornate hats. Mr. Parris drove the cart off the main street and down a small byway.

John and I stood wide-mouthed in the back room of

the milliner shop. It was filled with colored cloth. There were boxes of buttons, laces, and yarns. In one corner was a huge weavers loom. Two forms shaped like the bodies of women stood draped with nearly completed gowns.

Dazzling Juliet DuVille entered. She saw me admiring the cloth. "Beautiful silks and wools from London and Paris," she said. She wore a dress of deep green in a soft fabric I had never seen before. Its color matched her striking eyes. "We furnish everything to make gentle ladies beautiful and vain."

She floated over to John. "You will do all the heavy lifting, pick up shipments from the docks and help with deliveries." She turned her attention to me. "Do you sew?"

"I think I could do that," I pointed at the weaver's loom. I'd had a little experience with the loom in Barbados.

"Lovely."

I picked up orange and blue yarn from a basket full of colorful choices.

"The colors of the sky, the ocean, and tropical flowers. They must look familiar to you."

I remembered what Mrs. Pearsehouse had said about people being people wherever they were. I felt hope. "I can use this?"

"Absolutely."

"If you have grasses, I can make baskets as well."

"I will get what you need."

I smiled.

Mr. Parris rented a small shop a short distance from Mrs. DuVille that he filled with things he brought back from his father's plantation in Barbados. To this, he added items of tin and porcelain from local makers.

At the end of our workday with Mrs. DuVille, Mr. Parris would come to her shop and walk us to his shop to work another few hours for him. I wiped clean the shelves while John stacked new items upon them.

Two ladies walked into the store and perused the items there.

"May I assist you?" Mr. Parris asked.

"My mistress sent me down to see if you have some white table linens. We need some for tonight."

Mr. Parris went to a high shelf and pulled down a stack of linens.

"How many can I wrap up for you?"

"How much? I hear that you find your stock a bit too precious."

"These are very fine Irish linens, hand embroidered on the edges." He held the edge of the cloth up for her to see. "Very nice," he said and then Mr. Parris named his price.

One of the ladies made a *humphing* noise at the back of her throat as they walked out.

I could see that Mr. Parris wanted to run after her, but he did not.

I sat at the loom creating a colorful pattern in wool. It would be a light blanket that could be thrown over the knees of a lady as she rode down the street in a carriage.

I pulled a new skein of yellow from a basket I had made. The basket had a pattern of tiny brown frogs around the lip. A stack of other baskets sat nearby.

Mrs. DuVille had allowed me to make myself a new dress with a warm jacket to wear. I also made sleeping mats and blankets, mostly from remnants, for John and I to take to Mr. Parris's house to lay out by the fire.

Mrs. DuVille entered with a small, silver-serving tray. On the tray were small round balls.

"Try one," she said, a delighted look on her face. She

set the tray on a table near me. "These are wonderful."

I hesitated and then took a candy. I slipped it into my mouth. Its sweetness melted on my tongue. Instantly, I saw in my mind the backs of men, scared and broken, as they worked the cane in Barbados.

"I'm considering serving these to my ladies. What do you think?"

"They will like these," I agreed.

"My ladies love your colors and patterns." She touched the edge of the basket appreciatively.

As she turned her gaze from me, I spit the sweet from my mouth.

Mrs. DuVille ran a hand over the fabric on the loom. "You're a godsend."

I looked down. "Thank you, Ma'am."

"Would you like another?" Mrs. DuVille held out the tray to me.

"They're very good." At her insistence, I picked a second sweet and hid it in my hand until I could slip it into a bit of leftover fabric for which we had not yet found a use. I made as if I wiped my palm with the fabric and then slipped it into my pocket.

Mrs. DuVille sat in a brocade chair and slipped a candy into her mouth. She said, "You'll make me rich if I can steal you away from Mr. Parris."

Mr. Parris introduced us to a frail woman with skin the color of bleached seashells. She was a simple woman who followed Mr. Parris's every lead, as if she had no will of her own. Her expression was often one of bewilderment. Ms. Elizabeth Eldridge had become Mrs. Samuel Parris.

John unloaded more trunks and boxes, these belonging to the new Mrs. Parris. I could not imagine what was contained within or where we would put them within Mr. Parris's small wood and stone space.

As John set down the final crate, Mr. Parris pried open the box. Mr. Parris pulled out plates, pitchers, and other stoneware. When he found two silver candlesticks, he put those into a burlap sack.

Later that night, we heard Mrs. Parris speak to her husband in a tone that she had saved for when they were alone. She asked him about this taking away of her things.

"You're a lout," Mrs. Parris said.

He flew from the rooms leaving her crying quietly in the back.

"Must he take my finest things?" Mrs. Parris asked, not really directing her comment to anyone.

"What makes a silver candlestick more valuable than a wooden one?" I asked. "Both do the job of holding the candle."

Mrs. Parris looked startled as if I were a flock of birds flushed from the trees. She took me in for a moment before she fled the room.

6
Boston, June 1688

If there was one thing that I had learned in the eight years John and I had lived in Boston, it was that you had to be prosperous to live in this culture and Mr. Parris was not. The English seemed to think that accumulating land and property—things that could be made, grown, traded, and shipped to be sold—brought them high status. They erected bigger and bigger buildings with locks and keys to protect their accumulated wealth. To me, it seemed that their things did not enrich them, but enslaved them.

Mr. Parris had brought many items into their home in Boston. These included some of the things I had seen in the hold of the ship: silver serving trays and candlesticks, a fine rug for the floor, an ornate clock; but these things had begun to disappear until only the most functional objects remained.

Mr. Parris called himself a merchant, but so far as I could tell Mr. Parris made nothing. He was not a hunter or a fisherman. The woods and oceans were full of food, but the Parris family had none.

Beyond the shops or the regular market days, there was nowhere Mrs. Parris or I was allowed to gather wood or berries or herbs. Houses and roads had taken the place of wild food in the woods.

Mrs. Pearsehouse dressed too flamboyantly and was too outspoken. Mrs. DuVille owned a business and supported a secret boy who was a secret from no one. Neither Mrs. Pearsehouse nor Mrs. DuVille would be considered proper English women, but Mrs. Parris would. While Mrs. Parris would have words with Mr. Parris in their private quarters, she never did or said anything other than what he would find acceptable in public. She stayed at home and did needlepoint or wrote long letters to family and friends she had left behind. Other gentlewomen came to tea or she would visit them. Once a week, when she felt herself well enough, she and John would call on the sick and poor. What seemed to me to be the only bright spot for her were market days. She loved market days.

We carried baskets and walked among the merchants and traders. They called their hellos to Mrs. Parris and tried to lure her to their wares. Mrs. Parris smiled and nodded in return.

Mrs. Parris had not been out of the house since the birth of her third child, Susannah. Friends stopped her and they whispered in contained tones about trouble for James II in England and what that might mean for the colonies. No matter how dire the subject, Mrs. Parris could not contain her happiness at being out among people.

"Tell me about your homeland?" I asked Mrs. Parris.

"England?" Mrs. Parris paused to consider some ears of corn. "It's a lot like here. God knows the men have worked hard enough to make it the same."

"Then why did you come?"

"If you mean me, no one asked for my counsel. If you mean all the English, my answer would be more complicated."

Mrs. Parris put several ears of the corn in her basket. I waited unsure if she intended to answer.

"Men in England have been fighting about religion for longer than I can remember. One group held that the king had divine rights given to them by God. They tended to believe in the established church and were primarily the rulers and rich landowners. Another group wanted to reform the church and make government more accessible to all. They tended to be people like merchants who thought there were other ways besides owning land to make money."

"Who thought of this idea that land could be owned?" This idea was far from my comprehension.

Apparently, it was not clear to Mrs. Parris as well. She walked off into the crowd to greet a nearby vendor.

I made the ingredients that Mrs. Parris and I brought home go as far as possible, but the Parris family was hungry.

John and I ate a good midday meal each day with Mrs. DuVille who took pity on us. She traded beautiful baskets and shawls that I made and so did not begrudge us some food. She said we couldn't work if starved.

We had been all over each other in the Parris's rental space, so Mr. Parris had bought a larger house after Betty was born. The Parris household had grown to include seven year old Thomas, Betty, who was six, and baby Susannah. The Parris family depended on the small amount of income Mrs. DuVille regularly put in Mr. Parris's palm. Mrs. DuVille offered more than once to buy us, but Mr. Parris repeatedly refused.

When Mr. Parris bought a small native boy, I suspected that his slaves were considered a large part of his wealth. This boy was small and afraid, but he was big enough to make it on his own.

Several months before, Mr. Parris, John, and the boy were visiting a church in a nearby town. The town was on the edge of a wood that the boy recognized and John believed the boy could find his way. While Mr. Parris was inside the church, John simply turned his back and the boy walked away. Mr. Parris was furious and made John search for the boy for hours to no result, but Mr. Parris was too afraid of John to beat him as he looked like he wished he could.

I set food on the table for the family. Mr. Parris read from the Bible and then led the family in prayer, something he had only recently begun to do. The family ate too quickly and in uncomfortable silence.

Finally, I made small plates for John and I and we sat by the hearth in the corner of the room to eat. Mr. Parris tapped his foot at a furious pace as he glared at us.

"You grow fat as we grow lean," Mr. Parris pointed a long finger at me. "You steal from my table."

"No sir." I was alarmed at the accusation.

He grabbed my plate of food and swept its contents onto Thomas's plate. He did the same with John and Betty. Mr. Parris left us and stormed down the hall to his office. He slammed the door.

"The weather was fine today." Mrs. Parris spoke of anything but their hunger. "I heard the men speaking of a cold snap to come." I understood. Mr. Parris was desperate to feed his family and angry that he could not.

After the family retired and the house was quiet, Betty came to us. She nestled into my arms and I soothed her. Mr. Parris did not believe in such coddling, so I tried to be as quiet as possible.

John opened a small bundle he had brought from our meal at Mrs. DuVille's. He gave Betty a few bits of bread and a slice of cheese.

"No," Betty said. "You keep it. Papa took your dinner."

"It's for you," I said. She needed no more encouragement. She ate.

Mr. Parris opened his office door. He sat behind his desk fuming as he listened to me cooing to his child, soothing his child and feeding his child when he could not. I knew he was there and did not care. I leaned toward John and in a breath that barely left my throat, I whispered, "Something must be done."

It was quiet and Mrs. DuVille was out. John and I ducked into the alley behind the milliner shop. The day was getting long, but it was not yet night. I stripped my apron, cap, and neckerchief. I pulled my necklace of feathers and seeds from under my collar to show at my neck.

John stripped to the waist. He shook a makeshift rattle made from an old squash gourd. I chanted and danced.

Mrs. DuVille rushed out the back door. She looked horrified. "What are you doing?"

"We have no shaman, so John calls the spirits that inhabit all living things."

"For what purpose?"

"To safeguard us. Mr. Parris doesn't have enough food and it makes him angrier and more fearful each day."

"No. John, you must stop." Mrs. DuVille laid a hand on John's to bring his movement to a standstill. "You can't do this."

"We have no shaman," I said. "We must call…"

"No. No. No," she said. "Neither of you. You must never do this again. People won't understand. Promise me. Never again."

I wanted to protest, but did not.

Mrs. DuVille gave me a little hug. I didn't know what to make of this until she said, "Mr. Parris has contemplated a change in career. He has been acting as substitute for ministers who must be absent from their duties. Soon, he will become the Reverend Parris. He's been given a parish in the village of Salem."

"We leave Boston? We leave you?"

"It's farm country. The congregation pays the minister with food. At least you won't be hungry."

Dread pierced my heart.

7
Trek to Salem Village, June 1688

Mr. Parris loaded the household into a wagon hooked up to his old nag. That included Mrs. Parris, Thomas, Betty, and baby Susannah. The family huddled together under a light blanket for the nearly forty-mile ride from Boston to Salem Village.

The back of the wagon was loaded with household goods, so John and I stood beside it. Mr. Parris clicked and the aging horse slowly moved the wagon. The horse hardly looked able to haul the wagon's current load. It was clear that John and I were expected to walk behind.

We took a road that went along the Atlantic Ocean. A brisk wind whipped through our clothes and bits of sand stung our skin. Dunes covered with wispy grass blocked our view of the sea. Gulls with black backs and white breasts flew overhead. Soon, I had to struggle to keep up with the wagon, so John lifted me into his arms and carried me along.

A settlement called Saugus in the distance measured our progress toward it. It was a small collection of buildings centered between what turned out to be a tannery and shoemaker. The pastor at the meetinghouse was inviting, but we did not stay. We refilled our water barrel and moved on.

Instead, we camped that night in the dunes another couple of miles down the road. John beat the foliage, a combination of grasses and flowering vines, for snakes. I laid out sleeping mats for the family and cooked the evening meal, but I was so exhausted from the trek that I didn't bother to eat.

I pocketed a piece of johnnycake for later.

John led me a short distance off, but still under the watchful eye of Mr. Parris. John wrapped us both in his cloak as we lay down and he laid my cloak like a blanket over us both. Sleep was fast in coming, but I heard Mr. Parris's final words to us.

"Gather some oysters in the morning," he said. "We'll take them with us."

I slept through the night.

I woke before the dawn sun and added fuel to kick up the embers of the fire. I prepared a pot with clean water ready for tea, but as the family was still soundly asleep I did not put it on.

John picked up a pail and a large wooden spoon. We walked along the shoreline. The oysters seemed most plentiful in coves where the water was brackish. We filled the bucket with fresh seawater and dug with our hands or the spoon. We stored the oysters in the wet in the bucket. It was muddy work.

It occurred to John first that we were alone on the beach. It was shaping into a warm and pleasant day. With a slow grin, John began to strip his clothing. He ran across the odd, rocky beach into the ocean. I disrobed to my shift and followed.

John was swimming hard out to sea and I was doing my best to catch up. All I thought about was the kiss that waited for me when I reached John. I thought about a genuine moment of solitude with him.

I hadn't thought about how cold the water would be in the Atlantic Ocean or how strong the tides. I was caught in a rip that was pulling me out to sea. I turned toward shore and swam with all my strength against it, but each swell of the water pulled me farther underneath. I bobbed at the crest, craning for a look at John, but I could not find him.

"John!" I tried to scream above the green water that bubbled from my lips.

I could hear Betty screaming or maybe it was the shrieking of the gulls.

Then the cramping in my side set in and I could no longer swim. I sunk below the surface where down was up and up was down. I saw a few small fish in the swirling brownish muck churned by the waves. I felt calm, peaceful. I wondered what would become of John when I was gone. I tried to imagine what it would be like to not live. I closed my eyes.

I picked up Yessi and tossed her far into the warm water. She floated for a few moments in the current and then began her swim in the warm river toward the shore.

A force caught hold of me, pulled me upwards to the surface. I gasped for breath.

Mr. Parris held me firmly with one arm as each of his strokes with the other arm moved us a tiny bit toward shore. John soon reached us and added his strength.

We landed panting in the shallows. Mr. Parris gasped at the shoreline. He had instructed his family to turn away from our supposed deaths. Only one of little Betty's blue eyes sneaked a look, horror in her expression.

"What do you think you're doing?" Mr. Parris yelled, his face red with fury.

When he had his wind, John stood and went to retrieve his clothes without answering.

I lay gasping a bit longer. I was finally able to struggle to my knees and then my feet. Waves crashed against my ankles and I wasn't sure I could take a step. I pointed to the pail of oysters.

"We got dirty," I replied.

Betty broke free of her mother's grasp and ran to me. Mr. Parris caught her up before she reached me and carried her to the wagon. Within the hour, we were ready to resume the journey to our new home.

We stopped for a day in Salem Town. We entered near the port, prosperous because of fishermen and shipbuilding. We moved past the center of town with houses built close together for protection, a mill, a blacksmith, and other smaller businesses. We traveled down Federal Street past the courthouse and the jail.

On a small lawn outside the courthouse, there was a man locked with his head and arms secured within three holes cut into wooden boards. Several people stood nearby, taunting and shaming him. One small boy was poking him with a stick.

Salem Town, like Boston, was crowded with pale people. It was a regret of my eight years in Boston that there were so few people of color like John and I. There was no community for us. No friends. No neighbors. No one.

I was not sorry when we left Salem Town behind. We took an inland road through woods of maple trees; their leaves red and yellow, flew in a flurry around us. The sun lit the veins of each one.

Salem Village was an annex of Salem Town. As we moved toward Salem Village, the forest called me back to another time. Vertical limbs sheltered the road, pitted and rutted. The road narrowed in its attempt to hold back the tall firs.

We passed beside a rushing river, tripping over boulders in its path. I saw a fish jump into the aroma of molded earth covered in toadstools and fallen needles and then back into the churning water.

Cattle grazed on sloping meadows of grass. A field of wildflowers broke into the trees by the road, offering a splash of color and horizon, breaking up the shadows of the forest. The field was made of rich, fertile land fine for growing maize, rye, and grass to feed the animals.

I allowed myself a moment of hope.

8
Salem Village, June 1688

The wagon made its way around a center square. The barkeep stepped out of his tavern on the common, a two-story plank building with beveled glass windows. It had two columns by the door and a small portico over the entrance.

The barkeep was a burly man, both large and tall, about a half-century in age. He followed our every step with his eyes. His look appeared neither interested or not. He rubbed his hands on his apron and went back inside.

As we passed people and they spotted our dark skin, they stopped what they were doing to stare. Some were curious, but overall, the look was definitely distrustful.

A man stepped from behind the tavern. This man put his hand on the knife on his belt. "Savages," he said to no one in particular.

Our wagon traveled a dirt road past a house on a patch of green grass surrounded by split log fence. A girl on the edge of womanhood exited the house. She was gangly and already bent from hard work. Her hair was limp and her skin had a ghostly pallor. She carried the look of someone haunted by angry spirits.

The girl caught John's aspect and went a paler shade of white. She screamed. Once she began, her screeches turned over to hysteria. I winced at the pitch and volume of her screams.

People rushed from their houses and the fields to see what they could do. Mr. Parris jumped down from the wagon.

"He's a slave, not a red Indian," he yelled as he ran toward the girl. "Not the same," Mr. Parris said quietly. "They are from Barbados. Peaceful. Never hurt anybody."

Not from Barbados, I thought.

A woman from the house came out and shoved Mr. Parris out of her way, somewhat disrespectfully to my mind. These people had just made him their spiritual leader. Did they not like him, trust him? The shaman of my village was the most revered person of the tribe.

The adult put her arms around the young woman's shoulder until the girl began to calm. The girl seemed stricken, hysterical, and self-involved, all at the same time.

Mr. Parris returned to his family and stood by the wagon.

"What was that about?" Mrs. Parris asked.

"Mercy Lewis. She's not been the same since her parents were murdered by the Wabanakis Indians in a raid about three years ago." Mr. Parris shook his head in disgust. He looked toward Mercy.

"How is it that you know these intimate things about this girl?" Mrs. Parris asked.

"Mercy Lewis was living with the Reverend George Burroughs when this was his post."

"Will she live with us?" Mrs. Parris sounded a bit alarmed.

"No. The Putnam family took her on. She is servant for them now."

Mrs. Parris looked worried. "Are there still Indians here about?" She looked around as if hostiles would be standing at the edge of the wood, so I looked as well. No Indians.

"There are a few small bands here and there on their own," Mr. Parris said.

"I thought the natives had been confined to the Praying

Towns," Mrs. Parris said.

It was Mrs. DuVille who had told me that the English arrived on this land on their ships from a far away place not more than three generations ago. Before then, only the native tribes lived here. They lived quietly on their ceremonial lands, traveled from place to place on foot and grew only enough food for the tribe. They had not seen white men or horses or guns ever before in their lives. I did not have to imagine what that would be like. I understood the fascination of seeing these curious pale men and the allure of their metal objects. I remembered.

Mrs. Duville had heard some stories about the natives. There had been a war between a great shaman named Metacon and his peoples against the English. At first, Metacon had many victories. This made him bold. But the English allied with natives who had been living in the English way in Praying Towns, where they were supposed to act like the English, and, when watched, they did. But the colonists didn't want to know the natives, didn't care what they did. They were left mostly alone, until needed.

Together, the English and the Indians from the Praying Towns separated Metacon from his food and weapons. One of these Praying Town Indians killed Metacon in battle and took his head as a trophy to the English.

Thousands of people, both English and Indian, had been killed in the war. Many of the Indians who did not die were sold as slaves in the West Indies. I remembered what that was like as well.

Mr. Parris read his wife's distress. He spoke to her, but slightly inclined his head toward John and I.

"God's salvation is determined prior to evidence. Some beings are just beyond it. We try to redeem the Indians, but as beings beyond God's favor, they have no faith in Christ.

Sometimes we just can't."

Mr. Parris had recently taken up this talk of God's grace and who was in it and who was not. When he knew he was hired to be an ordained minister, he went to visit his brethren and listened to their words. He imitated their speeches and actions, but I did not think that he felt it.

The wagon arrived at the parsonage. It was a small rectangular house with no gables. Instead the roof was steeply angled off the back to allow rain and snow to run off. There were four small windows across the front—two on the tallest part of the top story and two on the bottom floor.

The bottom quarter of the house was made from local stones with a clamshell grout. The top was white hand-cut wood, grayed by weather. The house had a brick chimney in the center and a root half cellar with a lean-to on the east side. Firewood was neatly piled under the lean-to.

A stacked stone fence surrounded the property, pretending to keep at bay patches of dense woods. Several fields had been cleared and the topsoil waited to be turned for planting. A small stream bordered the land on one side.

Mr. Parris trudged a path around the borders of the land. His wife followed behind him. Mr. Parris seemed pleased with its aspect.

"Is it ours?" Mrs. Parris asked.

"Not yet. Negotiations continue." Mr. Parris's mood soured. "They lend us use of the parsonage and will pay our rate in firewood and crops."

Between the stream and the back door, the remains of a kitchen garden stood. Vines for beans withered on the ground. Brown stalks of maize bordered the back of the plot. John and I shared a look. I took heart by putting my hands into the earth. John kicked a clump of dirt and then picked it up. It was rich, dark, and aromatic.

The first floor had two large rooms separated by a great two-sided fireplace that dominated both rooms. The Parris parents unloaded a bed and set it at the back of the front room along with a small cradle for Susannah. A small settee was angled in front of the fire with a writing desk in the corner. The second room was a large kitchen that would hold an ample dining table with two long benches. On the back wall there was a large kitchen pantry and a steep ladder to a loft.

The children's loft had a long, tilted ceiling. There were the two windows on its only vertical wall that would allow some airflow in the warm months, but also had heavy wooden shutters that could be closed in the cold months. The girls, for we had been told that Betty's cousin Abigail Williams would soon come to live with us, would share a bed on one side. Thomas had a bed on the opposite.

There was a good amount of discussion between the Parris parents about what to do with the slaves. Mr. Parris did not want John and I in the house, but Mrs. Parris pointed out in a practical manner that we would freeze to death outside—even in the lean-to. It was finally agreed that we would sleep in the pantry. It was a pantry of ample size with a wide center aisle. I spread our woven mats on the floor, happy to have walls and a door that separated us from the family.

I began my duties on the farm by tilling a patch to plant a garden. John helped by breaking the hard ground. I took a minute to watch him pulling rocks before I sowed a row of seeds. Chances were good the seeds would sprout into food.

Mr. Parris followed Betty as she chased a chipmunk into the woods. He lifted Betty and held her for a moment to his face, his hands large under her arms against her tiny back.

Six-year-old Betty was small for her age. Her eyes were pacific like the sea and her hair was shiny as the morning sun. By far her most unique feature was her full, red lips. She used them often in her ready smile. She was delicate and sweet and easy to love.

I watched as John jealously watched father and daughter.

Mr. Parris looked his way. "Are you thinking of having your own children?"

"We have no plan to have children," I said.

Mr. Parris nodded in accord with John.

"Unless it's God's will," John finished, using Mr. Parris's term for the grandfather.

Betty circled her arms around her father's neck. Mr. Parris twirled her in the air. There was a lightness to him that I had rarely seen. We were in a new place, a new beginning, away from his struggles in Boston. Mr. Parris had allowed himself to hope just as John and I had.

I had heard whisperings that not everyone in Salam Village wanted Mr. Parris. I understood that. I couldn't see how you could declare yourself spiritual leader without studying the ancient teachings and learning the traditional ceremonies and rituals.

John came and stood close behind me, so that I could feel his manhood on my backside.

"He looks happy," John remarked.

I slipped my hand behind my back to touch him. "I fear it will not last," I said.

"Children bring such happiness to a family," John said, ignoring my comment.

I dropped my hand and returned to my work.

9
Salem Village, November 1688

On the last Sunday of the month of November, Mr. Parris was ordained as a Christian minister by the town's previous pastor, the Reverend Nicolas Noyes. The community watched him receive a benediction by the Reverend John Hale. He was now the Reverend Parris and his goodwife was named Goody Parris as all married Puritan woman were called.

Reverend Parris spoke from his heart about fresh beginnings, setting aside the divisions of former times, and moving forward to a future of tranquility and unity. His heart seemed warm and a few of his flock nodded their heads in agreement.

After, the whole community came together around tables and benches placed under large trees nearly stripped of their foliage by the coming of winter. The dead leaves of red, yellow and brown protected the damp soil as they nourished the tree's roots.

With the exception of the ladies' white coifs, my royal blue shawl was the boldest splash of color in a sea of gray and brown clothes. Most of the women wore a short cape that cut the chill over their waistcoat, petticoat, and apron. The fabrics used varied to show the wealth of each household, with my dress being the most plain. I had no fancy collar or cuffs, but my outfit was clean and well stitched as I had made it myself.

Each of the men removed a tall felt hat from his head. Their doublets and ruffs revealed that these jackets, as were the women's clothes, were their Sunday best.

First the men sat and then the women served a chestnut soup with roasted turkey, maize, and a root vegetable. The root, called potato, was introduced to the English by the local Indians before the natives understood what they had to fear.

After serving, the women joined the men. The slaves and servants stood behind. We would eat the remains later.

As in Boston, the Reverend Parris had rented out John, this time to Nathaniel Ingersoll who owned the tavern. Like Boston, this resulted in twice the work for John as he still did many tasks for the Reverend Parris.

Mr. Ingersoll handed John a pitcher of beer. John walked from man to man around the two large tables and filled each cup.

Dr. William Griggs welcomed the Reverend Parris with a warm two-handed shake as he sat on the bench beside the man.

"Welcome, sir," Dr. Griggs said.

Betty hung on the back of her father's neck and son Thomas sat beside him. The Reverend Parris patted Betty's hand affectionately as he rose to speak.

The group settled. The Reverend Parris lifted his hands and eyes in silent and reverent prayer. His expression was beatific and affected. After this moment, he took Thomas's hand on one side and Betty's on the other. Mrs. Parris held Susannah in her arms.

"Take the hand of a loved one, friend or neighbor," the Reverend Parris said. A tentative smile cracked his face.

People shifted to stand and take their neighbors hands. I took hold of John.

"Thank you, Lord, for the safe arrival of my family in Salem Village. Thank you for the opportunity to meet so many new friends and neighbors."

As his prayer went on, Betty pulled her hand from her

father's. His eyes followed Betty as she crossed the lawn to me. Betty smiled at me with her soft red lips. She looked young for her age, but she had a sweet disposition and intelligent eyes. She crowded near to me and took my hand in her small thin one. I wanted to stroke her hair, but dared not.

Betty shivered; I didn't know if from the cold or her desperation for attention. I couldn't stand it. I gathered her in and wrapped my shawl around her thin shoulders.

The Reverend Parris's face turned from sublime to an angry snarl as he watched me with his daughter. I let go of Betty and pushed her away. She whimpered like a hungry puppy.

Goody Mary Sibley moved next to Goody Sarah Osborne. "I've brought a special tea I've prepared to help ease your distemper."

Goody Osborne had been feeling ill of late, so she smiled and accepted the well-meant package.

Goody Sibley left to make a plate of food for Goody Osborne.

Goody Sibley was a gentlewoman, one of the wealthiest in town. While most of the women wore homespun, Goody Sibley had a collection of fine silks. Today, Goody Sibley wore a forest green gown with velvet sleeves, likely imported from Europe. It reminded me of a fabric in Mrs. DuVille's shop, something I had not seen among the rough woven clothes most women wore in Salem Village. She was soft on the inside and outside. She was gregarious and gracious, but she still managed to somehow keep herself aloof. No one really knew Goody Sibley.

Dr. Griggs sat down near Goody Osborne as Goody Sibley returned and set down the full plate of food.

"Isn't that nice. Eat up. You must keep up your strength," Dr. Griggs told Goody Osborne.

Betty cautiously crept back toward me. I shooed her toward Goody Parris and moved near Goody Osborne. I lifted the package to my nose and smelled the strange herbs inside. I glanced at Goody Sibley.

Was she a shaman? I wondered. Did they have a female shaman in this strange, new place?

10
Salem Village, April 1689

Goody Parris sat on an old wooden chair by the back door sunning herself as I weeded around the small corn stalks that had recently appeared in the soil. I had planted tomatoes, potatoes, beans, and strawberries, but the New England winters were long and the soil was rocky. So far, these plants had not appeared.

I dripped a little water from my fingertips to the place where the strawberries had been planted. I did this every sunny day to keep the soil moist, but not wet. I started the seeds over a month ago inside near a window, setting them in damp soil. When the seed split and put out a sprout, I moved them to the cold ground, careful so that it was unlikely to freeze again. I was most disappointed that the strawberry plants had not yet grown. I remembered strawberries from my days working for Mrs. Pearsehouse. Mrs. DuVille had strawberries a few times as well. Strawberries were a favorite of mine.

I saw Goody Sibley slip into the deep forest on her own. I had determined by keeping an eye on her that Goody Sibley understood the natural world. I couldn't stop myself from following her.

"I think I see some mushrooms," I called to Goody Parris who lazily waved me on.

Goody Sibley carried a near empty basket. She stopped to rub the plants she found on the way between her fingers. She smelled the tips of her hands. After careful inspection, she placed a variety of barks and leaves into the basket.

I put some of these same leaves into my cap. The plants were unfamiliar to me, but I wished to know more.

Goody Sibley exited the well-worn path and entered a remote and thickly grown portion of the woods. She paused from time to time to admire the new green leaves at the tops of the trees. This color brought a smile to her face.

Goody Sibley stopped beside a stream. She sat beside the water and dug in the earth until she had created a deep hole. From her basket, she removed a cloth packet from the bottom, hidden under a thick layer of plants. She placed the packet into the earth and covered it with dirt. She mumbled words that I could not hear. Over the top, she returned the dirt and stacked stones into a pyramid.

"Are you a shaman?" I asked.

Goody Sibley startled, surprised to find me there. "What?"

"You seem to know the plants. Do you believe in animal spirits too?"

"Why do you ask these things? Did the Reverend Parris send you to me?"

"No." I was made nervous by the question. "I would never...I see your connection to the earth." I stammered a bit over my words, now uncertain of what I'd said.

"What do you want?"

"I want to learn." I reached into her basket and pulled out a few thick stems of serrated leaves. The shiny bronze leaves felt a bit leathery and each stem had a cluster of pale pink flowers. The stems clutched dirt in their roots and shoots. "Huckleberries," I said. "What will you do with these?"

"I will try to plant them in my yard."

"Will that work?"

"Possibly."

"What do they do?"

"The fruit makes a nice jam," she responded, still with wariness in her voice.

"Yes," I said showing my interest.

"And a wine," she added.

"I would guess that they make a purple or black dye."

Goody Sibley relaxed for a moment. "You're truly interested in plants."

"Yes, but there are so many here I don't recognize."

Goody Sibley held up the huckleberry vine. "When mature, they strengthen the blood."

I smiled.

"Good for the hair and skin as well."

I picked up a second plant. "And this? I hear it being called worthless, a weed."

"Every plant has value."

"So I've always believed as well."

"You must not say these things or the reverend will name you a pagan or worse a witch."

"A pagan?"

Goody Sibley was discomforted. "Such talk could have a very bad result. More horrible than you can imagine."

"Regardless of whether you teach me or not, you can count on my discretion. I will say nothing. You have my word." Goody Sibley relaxed at my words, so I ventured one more question. "What is a pagan?"

"Best I can tell, it is a description for anyone who believes differently than in the Christian's one true God."

"And witches?"

"They say witches harken after Satan, but often it's just an excuse for punishment. They go to great pains to bring offenders to confession and repentance."

I couldn't help but notice that she said "they" when referring to the Puritans, not "we."

"In Dorchester, there was a woman who was executed as a witch, but in truth she was merely a single woman who had played the harlot and grew with child."

"They killed her?" I asked, horror in my tone.

"I've heard of a woman in Charleston who was executed for having angry words with her neighbor. There have been a handful of similar situations. "

"Are witches always women?"

Most recently a man named John Godfrey from Andover was named a witch. He was known to be very litigious. His last case was dismissed. He sued his accusers and won, but then he was named as evil."

"You don't believe in evil?" I asked.

Goody Sibley stood and brushed the dead leaves from the back of her skirt, so I also stood.

"We best be getting home," she said. "You'll be missed."

11

Salem Village, June 1689

Since I couldn't find the jungle plants with which I was most familiar in the woods of Salem, Goody Sibley made a potion for me to help deter pregnancy. She was happy to do so, plus she did me the service of not expressing in words her reasons for helping me.

As for me, I had convinced myself that I did not wish to have babies. A slave baby was not my own. The baby was property that could be torn from me at any whim. I had experienced a like pain and never wished to do so again.

Goody Sibley made a small fire in a clearing by the stream we had visited many times now. It was our private place in the woods. She macerated leaves in a mortar and pestle she had brought with her for that purpose. It reminded me of my father who used two flat stones to accomplish the same thing.

"Are you concerned about the parentage?" Goody Sibley asked. She must have seen the obvious upset on my face.

"What's your meaning?" I asked.

Goody Sibley examined her feet closely. She was embarrassed and soon her implication came to me.

I was quickly getting into the habit of speaking with Goody Sibley about topics dangerous to me. Goody Sibley, being one of the wealthiest women in Salem, knew little of danger. I worried that if she repeated this one, the Reverend Parris would do worse than sell me, but I trusted her anyway.

"When we first came into Boston, John took Goody

Parris and the children on an errand at the master's demand. They planned to be gone most of the day."

"Parris sent them off so he could have his way with you?"

"Yes. But he did that only once. We reached an unspoken accord. "

"Accord?"

"He never touched my person again and I never put white snakeroot into his food again. He had bad breath, stomach pains, muscle stiffness, and vomiting for a fortnight."

Goody Sibley snickered.

"I promised him that if he touched me in an inappropriate manner a second time, he would not survive his next meal."

John and the family had returned home much sooner than the reverend expected. Goody Parris entered the kitchen door first, clearly surprised to see me, not as she expected me, but at the difficult task of making butter. She could see from the thickness of the cream at the top of the churn that I had been working on it for at least two hours. I cranked the churn's handle.

The reverend had been in the privy, but entered the house from the front and came into the kitchen.

John filled the kitchen doorway with a countenance more dark than I had ever seen. His eyes spat fire. His fingers curled and uncurled around an ax in his hands.

I had not planned to tell John of the events of the day. I knew that he would feel shamed that I had planned for this contingency when he had not, but one glance made it clear that all parties fully understood the situation.

John was thrown. He had been ready to murder the Reverend Parris and live with whatever came his way as a result of it. I forced a smile to my lips and softly said his name.

He took my face into his left hand and examined my skin left and right. Still clutching the ax, he lifted the fabric of my dress from my arms and examined those as well.

John backed out the door. He went to the woodpile and began to swing the ax. John was forced more often than he could stand to push down his emotions. God help anyone who attempted to separate him from that ax at this moment, but I went outside to him. I could unquestionably tell that the Reverend Parris was terrified. I had to calm down John. I watched him swing the ax until his upper lip glistened.

"John," I said.

In a moment, he paused. "I would die to protect you."

"I know that." I touched his arm with one hand while pulling the ax from his other hand.

"I would do anything."

"And I for you. I love you."

John's arms circled mine.

John and I didn't speak often of love. It was just there, a constant that did not need to be acknowledged. Looking back, I wondered if that was the first time I'd said the words. I was lost in this line of thinking when Goody Sibley spoke.

"Did he keep his promise?" Goody Sibley asked. It took me a moment to realize that she was referring to my accord with the reverend.

"He did."

It had not occurred to me before that he was not obligated to do so. I was his property. He could do with me as he wished. It was a new realization. The Reverend Parris was a man of his word.

John was one person with me and another with everyone else. With me, he spoke about things easily and told me everything in a faithfully true manner. With others, he spoke not at all. He felt that voice conveyed who you were. He said that silence was his power. When given a command, he wordlessly did it, without even a nod to the issuer, but he saw things, heard things, understood things.

John was smart. He seemed to be going about his business dully and seemingly without interest, but he listened to the conversations in the tavern and understood their content, especially as he learned different languages with ease. He had perfect English, a little French and words in several Indian dialects. He made determinations about who might be a friend and who might hurt us. He told me these secrets in the quiet of the night.

And John was strong. Consistent with his tribe, he wasn't as tall as some of these European men, but he was much more solid with taut muscles that did his bidding. John's countenance—along with the striping of overlapping scars on his skin—made even the strongest white man seem afraid of him, so in public John wore loose clothing that belied his strength. But in private moments, he was pleased by the failure of white men's efforts to beat him down. I'd run my fingertip over his patchwork of lines and wondered at the beautiful, proud, and strong man who was my husband. It sometimes seemed wrong not to continue his line. A baby would make him so very happy.

Back in Barbados, John had refused to speak to me for three days when I first told him that I didn't intend to have his children. He was angry, but didn't feel that he had the right to be as he never once mentioned babies in the first year we were together. After our loving became a regular event, his mentions became casual and frequent until I could ignore them no longer.

John had retreated into himself to worry out an answer. He did not speak to me for many days. I saw him speak to the Taino shaman. That night, he came to me with a gris-gris bag.

"Are you saying that you no longer wish to have relations with me?" he had asked.

"No," I said, shocked at the very idea. He was my solace. He was my comfort.

I could hear the drums beating out a rhythm outside our hut. He flexed his shoulder muscles and held his head high.

"You have your ways. Now I have mine. We will leave this decision to the grandfather."

He had stripped his loincloth and stood before me wearing only the gris-gris bag and several colored clays around his privates.

I laughed.

He gave a primal yell and jumped to me.

He yelled out in much the same way and swung me around in the air when I told him that Goody Sibley's brew had not worked. I told John in the morning, when my queasiness left little doubt.

"You won," I called out to him as I hung my head over our private piss pot.

John was in the kitchen. I joined him there, seeking a drink to clear my throat. I poured a little water from a pitcher into a cup. I swished the water in my mouth and spit it out.

He stopped mid-step when he took my meaning. He strutted around the kitchen like a cocky rooster, so proud of himself. His dance done, he kissed my face and neck. He cupped my sore and swelling breasts in his hands.

"Stop," I said. "I'm foul." My face must have reflected the worry I was feeling.

"Are you really so awfully against it?"

I could not save my child from a life of slavery. Now, all I could do was love and protect my baby. I touched my still flat womb and smiled. I realized as I said it, "Possibly not." It was as if those many worries had never been. They had no substance.

John placed his hand over mine. "Hello, my son," he said.

Mr. Ingersoll packed several furs and some metal works from Boston. He had heard of a small band of Indians camped several miles away and he wanted to see if they would trade for fish, beans, and squash.

Mr. Ingersoll had a Bible that had been translated into the Massachuset language. He packed it as well so that he could teach the heathens a little English and how to live based on the Bible's writings.

I sat on a bench in Mr. Ingersoll's tavern. I had brought a few of John's things for him to take. My life was changing too fast. My emotions flew up and then fell down at every turn. Thoughts and feeling clouded my mind. I could not think correctly. All I knew was that I didn't want John away from me while I was with child. But he had no choice, and so he went.

While John was away, I filled my day with routine. I cooked. I cleaned. I worked in the garden. I cared for the reverend's children. My feet felt heavy with fatigue. Each day seemed more difficult than the last. I waited none too patiently for John to come home.

When John returned he told me stories of his trip in an excited voice. He said that when Mr. Ingersoll arrived at the summer camp, he learned these people were some of the few remaining Wampanoag who had not died of white man's illness.

"At first landing many years past," John said, "Wampanoag had had more than forty villages." John held his arms wide. "But now there aren't enough remaining tribesmen to fill one village."

Mr. Ingersoll feared a feverish death, so he sent John with the goods and Bible. John couldn't read and Mr. Ingersoll knew this, but he felt that he shouldn't trade with the Indians without bringing Christianity, if only for appearance sake. Mr. Ingersoll waited for John a cautious two miles away.

John liked the Wampanoag. Its members were part of the People of the Dawn tribe, meaning that they came from the east. They got on just fine without words in the beginning.

John told me that, at the start, the People had been a trusting tribe who had been pleased to teach the English colonists how to grow crops and to fish the local waters.

"But, as sickness took more and more of them, the Wampanoag abandoned their villages and retreated to a coastal island. There are six or seven families of kinsmen who left the island to return to their old ways. They're like us."

Instead of focusing on teaching the People English, John worked hard at picking up more of their language. He soon had a good working vocabulary.

"I made a friend," John said. "His name is Ahanu. It means He Laughs. Ahanu is a warrior, a hunter and a fisherman. He wore clothing so soft. Ahanu said it's made of white tail deerskin and harbor seal pelt decorated with small white shells."

I thought of my moody and unhappy days while John was gone. I wanted to smile at his pleasure. I wanted to but could not.

"Ahanu has a new wife and she's as pregnant as you."

Ahanu's bride had put some maize and a pumpkin into a baby blanket she had made and sent it home with John for me.

Mr. Ingersoll didn't even bother to go on the next trip to the tribe. He sent John on his own.

I made a basket decorated with a spotted jaguar stretched along a thick branch. The jaguar was my spirit animal.

The shaman had said the jaguar symbolized my bravery and fearlessness. I wanted Ahanu and his woman to share that. I filled my basket with last year's chestnuts, sweet basil, and mint from my garden. When John returned to the village, I sent instructions with him detailing ways that each item in my basket could be used for health and flavor.

The tribe's field was made of many small hillocks. Maize grew at the center and squash, pumpkin, and bean vines wove within and tumbled down the hill. The forest beyond was accessible and broken with sunlight. Ahanu told John that this was a result of the firing. Fires were kindled just beyond the gardens in the fall and again in the spring. The fires burned the small undergrowth. It made it easier to track their prey during the hunt and it killed the mice and insects that pestered the hunters and the hunted.

I remembered this from my youth. My people had farmed to grow the cassava to use or trade. We would cut down the trees and vines in a small area and then burn off the underbrush. We then mixed the ash with fish oil to make the soil strong.

Ahanu invited John to the autumn fire and to go hunting with his band. John convinced Mr. Ingersoll to send him to the tribe at the right time. John stole a few hours and went to the ceremony in preparation for the hunt. John wanted to be the hunter and not be stalked like the prey. He supposed that Ahanu felt the same. This idea haunted John and he began to speak more frequently of escape.

As Ahanu showed John how to make a bow, he said that he had kinsmen who had moved north of an invisible line to a place near Nova Scotia to start a new life. Ahanu had heard that life was better there and planned to go himself one day. John also began to dream of crossing the invisible line.

And this is how it went each time Mr. Ingersoll sent

John to trade with the People of the Dawn. I loved this woman I had never met. I ran my hand over the weave of her blanket and I could feel her heart in it. I knew this woman. I understood her. I began to want my baby to grew up with these people. I began to want things I had not thought of in years.

Ahanu invited John and I to share food and shelter with his tribe until we could all escape to the north.

"I spoke with their shaman," John said. "He is very high status and wears much wampon. He wants to help us." Ahanu had to meet with the sachem—that's their chief—and the council because we would be runaways. It would be dangerous for them, but safer for us. We'd fit in.

There was good and bad everywhere, just as Mrs. Pearsehouse had said. I began to store food and other needed things. I hid them in the shelves of our storage room, ready to pull down at a moment's notice.

"When the baby is born, that's when we'll go," I said, but I found it hard to believe that we ever would.

12
Salem Village, July 1689

The Reverend Parris's eyes followed me wherever I went as I served breakfast for the family. It was disquieting and unnerving.

I felt queasy, not from the simple meal of bread and milk that I was serving, but from the pungent smell of the family in close quarters before scant morning ablutions. I had begun violently reacting to this smell since I became pregnant.

I fled to the creek that ran close by and wretched on a tree. The Reverend Parris followed me outside. He glared at me from a distance for a minute before he came forward and laid his hand upon my midsection.

"How long?" he bellowed. At that moment, my baby delivered his first kick. The reverend's eyes raged like a fire out of control.

I jumped. I had hidden my condition from the Reverend Parris for as long as could be, but the roundness of my belly gave me away.

The Reverend Parris screamed out his anger. If he made intelligent words, I could not understand them.

The family ran out of the house, but at his signal, kept their distance. Goody Parris held off Betty until she was able to pass her to Abigail. She warily crept toward the two of us.

Soon, I saw John running from the far field. He reminded me of a hawk, swooping out of the sky, talons exposed. He looked ready to shred the skin from the Reverend Parris's body.

The Reverend Parris grabbed a shovel. When John reached him, he bellowed, "Dig a hole."

John's every muscle grew taut. He panted heavily. He was barely under his own control. He silently refused.

The reverend intended that John should dig a hole for my protrusion. He intended to lay me in it and whip me for growing with child.

Goody Parris cautiously approached. "I beg you. Don't do this," She pulled at her husband's arm.

He shook her off. He wished to whip me until the baby was no more, but John waited ready to physically pull him off and pummel him. The reverend was secretly afraid of John's power. They had an accord too. John would do the work as the reverend said so long as he did not cross a line. The line stood like a wall between him and the Reverend Parris.

"Another mouth to feed," the Reverend Parris said in frustration and resignation. He backed down.

Goody Parris guided him back toward the house.

I put my arms around John as much to hold him in place as to garner his comfort.

We could hear The Reverend and Goody Parris talking as they walked away.

"We will sell the baby," he said.

I suspected the Reverend Parris would have even more to fear from John if he mistreated of our baby. I held John's neck more tightly, but I could feel his readiness to attack.

"No. Who would want a baby?" Goody Parris responded calmly, rationally, with words she knew would calm him.

"Perhaps you're right. We will get a much better price later, especially if it's a girl, especially if she's pretty, yes, when she is fourteen or fifteen."

"Yes. We'll talk about this much later," Goody Parris

said.

A sinister gleam lighted his eyes. If not a promise, these words were clearly a threat to John, to me, to our family. It became clear that the Reverend Parris found that he liked this leverage he had over us.

13

Salem Village, January 1690

Soon it was time for my baby to come, but the baby did not. I worked hard in the fields. I turned the earth, pulling the weeds away from the growing plants. I milked the cow. I spun wool. The trick was to stay busy. I was rewarded with irregular spasms.

Late at night, I awoke in gut-wrenching pain. My bedclothes strangled my feet, likely from my own thrashing. I awoke my sleeping husband when I felt the first convulsions.

In my head, I heard the voice of the Reverend Parris repeatedly telling me that labor was women's punishment for Eve's sin of eating the apple in the Garden of Eden. The Reverend Parris often liked to tell stories to explain things that were beyond his understanding. Usually, I ignored him.

I wanted to go to the clearing in the woods, but I knew I would make it no farther than the Parris fence line. I calmed my mind, focused on my body, and spoke to the spirits, asking for a calm and peaceful delivery. In response, the pains came close together. I screamed.

"What can I do?" he asked, worry in his voice, but I had no voice or will to answer. I responded with panting breaths.

It was excruciating, but bearable, until the tearing began. I tried all sorts of positions to ease my effort. I tried to hold in the moans, but another scream escaped.

"Restrain yourself," the Reverend Parris yelled from his bed. "Be quiet."

In a few minutes, Goody Parris appeared at the door in her nightclothes and shawl. She brought a bowl of water and a cool, comforting cloth for my forehead.

"It will be fine," she said. "You will live. The baby will live." She understood what worried my head.

"It's wrong. Something's wrong." My legs shook from the exertion.

"Shall I send for Dr. Griggs?"

"No. Will you please send John for Goody Sibley?"

"Goody Sibley?" She was surprised by my request for a highborn gentlewoman. I could see that she doubted that Goody Sibley would leave her warm bed on a freezing night to attend a slave in a closet.

"It's her I want." A gush of warm water fouled my mat.

I had been crowning for some time when Goody Sibley arrived. Just the sight of Goody Sibley made me feel better. I tried to smile.

With each pain, I bore down and felt movement. Goody Sibley held the cloth over my mouth to help keep me quiet, but the pain was intense. She made me a tea with turmeric and ginger that caused me to feel a bit better.

"She must be cut," Goody Sibley said. She brought a small knife from a bag that she carried. She sliced me quickly so I had no time to consider it and soon I felt the passage of the baby's head. Goody Sibley cut the cord and cleaned out the baby's nose and mouth. She washed the baby's skin.

She was delivered.

Goody Sibley laid my baby girl down on my chest—skin to skin—and covered us with a blanket.

"John, would you get me some clean, fresh snow?"

In a couple of minutes, John returned with a bowl.

I caressed the baby's tiny back with one finger and my baby girl rewarded me with a small yawn. She tested the air with the tip of her tongue and I laughed a little at my own amazement. I could feel her toes flex and relax against my skin. The baby was warm, calming as she slept against me. I felt connection as the baby's breath became one with mine. We were not just attached. She was still a part of me.

"You look happy?" John said as he sat down close to me.

"I am."

"Are you truly?"

"Yes. I truly am."

A weight lifted from my relationship with John. John and I had too many other people against us for there to be tension with each other, so when we disagreed we kept it to ourselves. But now this issue was past and we were as one.

"What shall we name her?" John asked.

In Boston, when we first arrived in town from the ship, brick buildings rose into a gray sky from the frozen ground that surrounded me. I thought this was the way of this world. I thought I would never see blue sky or living things again until one day as Mrs. DuVille and I passed an empty, desolate space, I saw a spot of purple. It was a small, almost blue purple flower with five petals surrounded by bright green leaves. Purple, the color of creation.

Mrs. DuVille stood beside me staring at the flower as well. "It's a sign of spring renewal," she said. "They're called violets."

I touched a finger to my baby's tiny cheek. "Violet," I called her.

With this flood of emotion, I hardly noticed as Goody Sibley cleansed and desensitized me with the snow and then stitched together my privates. I fell into an exhausted sleep.

Yessi stood dripping wet on the shoreline. Tears mixed on her cheeks with the water that fell from her black hair. She searched the river with her eyes until she found me on the deck of the ship. She raised both of her hands in farewell. Before she turned to go, another little girl joined hands with her. They both disappeared into the jungle.

I awoke, cried out and sobbed myself to senselessness.

14

Salem Village, April - October 1691

The spring sky was threatening and gray. Buds hung heavy on the trees from the weight of ongoing dampness. Every servant or slave in the community stood in the soggy fields. Mercy Lewis was to my right and another servant I did not know well was to my left. I ignored them. When I walked, my shoes sunk into sticky mud and pulled off from my feet. I removed them and left them where I stood. I continued planting down the long row. The hem of my long skirt turned to muck.

I paused for a few minutes to watch Dr. Griggs's young horses playing in a far field. There were a dozen or so prancing about, but only two held my attention. The horses became randy in the spring months. The mare would raise her tail and release a little water to show her interest to the stallion. The stallion would sniff, nip, and nudge the mare until she was ready.

In summer, lightning crossed the sky. I stood in the field where grain rolled like an ocean wave. I lifted a weary arm to blot sweat from my face. It was like standing inside a heavy cloud waiting to storm.

I noticed the Reverend Parris's loaned horse munching on a sweet, yellowish mucus on the rye. I rubbed it between my fingers, sniffed it, and then wiped it on my skirt. In a world of things unfamiliar to me, this was just one more.

Dr. Griggs had given the Reverend Parris one of the doctor's favorite horses for the reverend's use when his old mare had died. She was Dr. Griggs's horse, but Dr. Griggs let her stay in the Parris field. He wanted the reverend to be able to join him when a patient was so ill that they needed the reverend's ritual.

As it turned out, the Reverend Parris rarely joined Dr. Griggs on his rounds. It was Goody Parris who hooked up the cart and went when she felt well enough herself. She liked meeting and talking to the parishioners. Goody Parris would take John with her to ensure propriety with Dr. Griggs and in case she needed assistance.

Dr. Griggs liked John well enough. Dr. Griggs would talk with Goody Parris and John as they traveled. He let John ask a question from time to time. John wanted to hear about the continent across the ocean, a land that seemed more fantastic with each story telling.

"The world is large, much larger than you know. Beyond the European countries is Asia where slanted-eye people make silks and spices."

John knew that there was a limit to how far this relationship could go. He understood that from watching Dr. Griggs treat his own niece like a serving girl, but he wanted to know more.

"That's what they were looking for when they sailed to this shore, silks and spices."

"They got lost?" John was a slave because some sailors got lost.

Dr. Griggs laughed.

Dr. Griggs's grandfather had brought two Spanish horses over from England on the ship to the new world: a sire and a dam. They put the horses in a stall on the ship that was designed to protect warhorses. There were horses and cattle owned by others until each stall was filled. Uninvited, mice and rats also came along to the new world.

"The seas were rough and the voyage seemed unending. Can you image how horrified the horses must have been? They were sunk into a dark hold. They had no way to understand what was happening to them or how long it might last."

John did not mention that he did not have to imagine.

On the way home, John was made to walk so that Dr. Griggs and Goody Parris could whisper words that were not meant to be overheard, but John had extraordinary ears.

I watched the approach of the cart as I gathered stalks of rye, bent them back, and cut at the root. I moved on, bent back the next stalks, and cut again. And again. I gathered the cut grain and carried it toward the shed.

I crouched on the floor of the shed. It was little more than a lean-to at one end, with the other end a stall for the doctor's horse that protected her from the elements.

John brought the horse into its stall and brushed her down. He cooed in her ear as he worked. When done, he tossed a blanket across her back.

I used a mortar and pestle to thresh the rye, separating the grain from the straw. I covered my face with a shawl when I choked on the dust in the air. I felt heat in my body. My head throbbed. For a moment my vision blurred and I felt dizzy. It reminded me of my father's description of the sensation brought by the brew the Shaman used to open his mind to truth and meaning.

I noticed the strange kernels on the dried stalks and separated what I could. I thought of my father who warned that only a shaman could call the spirit world. I thought of Mrs. DuVille who warned never to attempt to do what was the shaman's role.

I crushed the strange kernels into the flour.

John watched for a moment.

I paused and looked up at him.

"The Reverend Parris has received many complaints from the parishioners," John said. "They aren't happy."

"This can't be a surprise."

"No. He argues with the selectmen. He tells them that he thinks this house and patch of land is his due and he will take it from them. The selectmen are angry and have decided to quit paying his wages."

I lifted my hand and let the rye that I had grown all summer sift through my fingers.

John nodded that I have understood.

I filled and stored the flour in burlap sacks that I stacked one on top of the other. I left the straw in a large pile on the floor to feed the horse.

Soon enough, I was in the kitchen kneading dough, turning it roughly over and over, letting it rise and bake on the hearth until the outer crust was crisp and brown, its warm aroma filling the room. It smelled so inviting. When the bread was baked, I put it into a large covered basket I had woven from local grasses.

Two-year-old Violet had grown like the rye in the fields and she never left my side. She was tall for her age like the rye stalk and her dark caramel skin had a touch of the sun in it. Her eyes were huge with extravagant dark lashes so thick it was almost as if she had an extra set.

I could spend my days doing little but watching her. My chest fluttered as if full of little butterflies with my love for her. I rocked her when she cried and fed her when she was hungry, just as I remembered my mother doing with my two sisters.

I pulled her unruly black hair into a topknot and strapped it with a bit of leather. She rewarded me with one of her ready smiles, her beautiful dark eyes deep wells of feeling.

I carried two baskets overflowing with bread to the Salem Village Common. Two-year-old Violet proudly walked behind me carrying her own little basket. Violet no longer wanted me to carry her.

Aya struggled in my arms to be put down on the ground. She pulled away and, when free, ran on her little legs.

From the baskets, I set warm bread in mounds down upon two rough wooden tables for Sunday feast. The community gathered under the large trees laden with fall color, leaves of yellow, red, and brown. The two tables stood apart, separated from each other. This division was new. I took my place behind the table with the Parris family.

Mr. Ingersoll handed John two pitchers of beer. John filled the cups on the first table. Someone from the other table took the second pitcher from John and they filled their own cups.

At the first table, the Reverend Parris, Mr. Putnam, and Dr. Griggs talked and laughed together. Thomas Parris dutifully sat beside his father while Betty wandered from table to table. The Reverend Parris rose. The group at his table settled. The Reverend Parris lifted his hands and eyes in prayer. He took Thomas's hand on one side and Mr. Putnam's on the other.

Nearby, Susannah struggled down from Goody Parris's arms. Susannah came to where Violet sat on the ground near an oak tree. Violet played with a doll. John had made the doll's face and body out of twigs. I made black hair, a yellow dress, and a little blue wrap out of scraps of yarn and fabric.

"Take the hand of a loved one, friend or neighbor," the Reverend Parris began.

People shifted to take hands. Just as Susannah reached for Violet's doll, I lifted Violet into my arms and took John's hand. Violet struggled in my arms. She wanted her doll. There would be trouble unless John and I made Susannah her own doll. I resented the fact that it would probably have to be better than Violet's doll.

"Thank you, Lord, for this bountiful harvest that will see many of us through the winter to come."

At the second table, the men and women sat in an almost silent, casual, but companionable way. They were a good distance from the first table. These were farmers and businessmen in the area who had objected to the village's request for their own church that was separate from Salem Town. They resented this greater autonomy from the town and they did not like the Reverend Parris, especially given his unrelenting request to have the parsonage deeded to him. Many, almost half the families who lived in town, did not attend the Reverend Parris's church. A good number attended no church at all rather than accept the Reverend Parris.

Strikingly handsome, William Porter sat with his family, including his father Joseph and uncle Israel. While most of the people of Salem had hair and eyes the color of mud, the Porters had hair the color of the sun and eyes the color of the tropical sea.

William was in his eighteenth year. I supposed I would have to start calling him Mr. Porter soon, but not yet. He had a compassion and intelligence beyond even his own relations who were known for such things. He smiled easily with teeth like bleached shells. William was lean and well-muscled from hard work. He moved fast like my spirit animal, the jaguar, but also knew when to halt and wait for life to come to him.

From the first table, Ann Putnam—who was just twelve—had her eyes on William Porter. Ann was snooty and entitled. Her mouth, both open and closed was the biggest thing about her. She was pretty in a privileged way, more from lack of work and expensive clothes than from any natural beauty.

Ann giggled with her friends Abigail Williams and Elizabeth Hubbard. Elizabeth leaned down and fed a bit of food to a stray dog that loitered around the table.

William Porter grabbed a loaf of bread and some white tail deer meat. I wondered what had become of the deerskin from the white tail deer. I would have loved to make a soft shirt like Ahanu's for John with it. I wished I could ask William, but I couldn't.

William walked to the edge of the wood.

Goody Sarah Good and her four-year-old daughter, Dorcas, stood partially hidden in the trees. They were ragged and had the look of the wild and homeless about them. Sarah's hair was long, bushy, and unkempt. Her face showed wear well beyond her years and she was missing a few of her teeth. She smoked a pipe that gave her remaining teeth and fingers a yellow coating. I had heard her called an old crone although she was clearly in her childbearing years.

Dorcas was a tangle of rags and curls. Her dress was a bit too large for her as if it was not made for her at all. Her skirt was filthy at the bottom from stomping down dusty paths and through fields and she gave off an unpleasant odor.

William Porter took the food to them. Without a word of thanks, Goody Good grabbed it from his hand and pulled the little girl into the trees.

William walked toward the well. Ann Putnam jumped from her bench and rushed to the well too, beating out Mercy Lewis by several steps. Ann drew water and handed it to William.

"Thank you Ann. Very thoughtful."

"You're welcome, William."

Mercy shot daggers at Ann. Ann smirked in return.

15
Salem Village, January 1692

The first truly foreboding sign was the plight of the Parris mare. The horse was dark brown like rich moist soil with a black mane and tail. The Reverend Parris described her as fourteen hands tall, average size but solidly built. The horse had another name, but the children called her Star because of the one white spot between her eyes.

Betty and Abigail patted Star and listened for the second heartbeat through her skin.

"It's like she has a rabbit inside of her," Betty said.

"A foul. That's a baby horse," Abigail explained.

Star had been off her feed for months. Star was heavy and hung low. Her hind legs swelled and she rocked to stay off of them. Her skin was hot and she produced no milk, even as the last days of her pregnancy approached.

At the first sign of cold weather, we moved Star into the barn until she was ready to foal.

It was a snowy night when the pains came. Dr. Griggs knew from the start that something was wrong. Usually, it took about thirty minutes of labor from when the feet first appeared to when the foal is born. Star was having a long and difficult birthing.

Star tried to foal for many hours. The sack that contained the foal was bulky and red as blood. The foal kicked and tore at the thick sack, but was too weak to break through. Star had remorseless contractions. She fell into spasms and screamed in pain as if her insides were being ripped apart.

I escaped from the barn and hid. It could have been me. I felt deeply for her.

Star and her foal died.

"I've never seen such a thing," Dr. Griggs said, a look of shock and shame on his face. "It's a bad omen."

Betty cried for a week and I wished I could join her.

Flakes of light snow swirled around my face as I lifted an armload of logs for the fire. My feet were frozen, heavy as stones.

In the distance, I could see Mercy Lewis carrying a heavy pack on her back. She passed the church as she made her way toward the Parris's parsonage.

We both kept an eye on the smoke swirling from the chimney as we moved toward the parsonage door. It promised warmth and comfort.

Mercy pushed me aside to enter first. She threw down her burden and moved to the fireplace in the main parlor.

Goody Parris lay sick in her bed. Her skin was as white as the snow outside. She rasped with each in-and-out breath.

Susannah lay in the bed beside her mother, her cries begging for attention. "Eat. Eat," Susannah repeated over and over.

"Rye," Mercy said. "To pay the minister's rate. Mr. Putnam said to bring it on."

Mercy worked as a servant for Mr. Thomas Putnam, Ann's father. Mercy had little more life to call her own than John and I since her parents were slaughtered in a raid between colonists and a rogue tribe. Mercy's life with the Reverend Burroughs was rumored to have been brutal, but of short duration. With the Putnams, Mercy lived on the cusp of the life she felt she was meant to have, but she could not touch it, feel it. She was not part of it.

I moved the heavy bag of grain into the other room, near the kitchen door. I would put it outside after I'd warmed by the blazing fire in the kitchen hearth.

"Thank you," Goody Parris said to Mercy. "Come in. The girls are in the kitchen."

Betty and Abigail sat around the loom as Ann Putnam worked a green wool fabric the color of deep forest.

"Tituba, tell us of your home," Betty said. "Tell us about the toad people."

"Not again," I let out a breath.

"Please." Betty took my hand. "Please."

I picked up Violet and held her in my lap. I rested my hand for a moment on her back feeling the steady rise and fall of her chest. I wanted to tell Violet the stories of my people and was pleased that Betty wished to hear them as well.

"We lived at the mouth of a mighty river, considered by many to be a mythical place," I started. "At the coldest time of the year, a ghostly fog would roll across the water and hide the trees. Then the toad people would crawl onto the shore. They would turn into little men who carried thunder and lightening with them."

"And they would play tricks on the fishermen."

"Yes. They would play tricks on our fishermen in their dugout canoes. The toad people would rock the canoes and tip them over. "

"The fishermen were in canoes in this weather?" Abigail asked.

"The coldest day was never this cold. There was no snow."

"But the toad people were invisible," Betty prompted.

"The toad people had big mouths and the inside looked like a basket or a sack. Many big things could fit inside. When the water level dropped, sometimes all we would find is a paddle or a net. And after that, it would grow warm and stay that way for the rest of the year."

"Where do the toad people live then?" Ann challenged.

"Under the lagoon."

"There are no toad people," she insisted.

"Of course there are. Who else brings the fog?"

"God?"

"Is God a trickster? No, it's toad people." I believed in toad people when I was a little girl, but my world had grown so much larger. I had experienced riptides and heard of whirlpools. It made me wonder whether my parents believed in toad people or if they were a symbol they used to talk about something unexplained.

"Is it really warm almost all of the year?" Betty asked.

I closed my eyes and pictured the jungle. "Yes. Warm. We swam every day surrounded by red, yellow, and purple flowers. Fruit grows in the trees." In my mind's eye, I saw my sisters playing in the mud and water on the shore of the river.

I shook the homesickness from my head. "Ann, that work is messy."

I picked up the pair of scissors she had been using. For a few moments, I could do nothing but stare at them. Scissors—a tool that had become commonplace in my life. In the jungle, I had used my teeth and they worked well enough. If I hadn't wanted scissors, I might still be there, at home with my mother and sisters.

"Take it out. Do it again," I said.

"I won't. I don't answer to you."

"Tituba," Goody Parris called from the main room.

I put a cup of tea and some squash soup with a bit of bread on a tray and took it into the parlor. I could hear the girls whispering as Abigail took an egg from a bowl on the table.

"Come out to the shed. I have something to show you,"

97

Abigail said. Abigail was the curious and adventuresome one.

"I was just starting to warm," Mercy whined.

Ann turned to the door. "You don't have to come."

Abigail and Ann went out the door. Betty and Mercy bundled up to follow.

After I left the tea with Goody Parris, I lifted the bag of grain and headed toward the shed myself. I avoided the horse stall and would not take Violet into the structure, but the girls buried themselves deeply into the pile of rye straw for warmth. Betty threw the straw into the air and danced as a fine dust billowed through the air on its way to the bare ground.

I stopped when I heard Abigail speaking.

"If you put an egg white into a glass of water, it becomes like a crystal ball. You can see your future." Abigail held the egg tentatively, so Ann pulled it from her hand and cracked it.

"I don't think you should," Betty said, but like the others she gathered around the glass.

"What's it say?" Mercy asked. "I want to be next."

"You're already living your future," Abigail said. "I'm next."

"I see the first letter of the name of the man I will marry. It's...." Ann paused for effect. "It looks like a "W." It is. It's William. It must be."

Mercy knocked over the cup with her hand. "It's a lie. And it's not Christian. I'll tell your parents that you're a pagan."

I returned to the kitchen just as Mercy and Betty ran in from the cold outside. Mercy removed her shawl. Betty sat at the table and pulled a chunk off a loaf of rye bread.

"Betty. Leave the bread alone. It's for dinner." I sat at the loom and began to undo Ann's work to repair it.

"Ann will marry William Porter," Betty said.

"How do you know that?"

"She saw it in an egg in a glass."

I stopped weaving and stood menacingly over Betty. I held a hand to my throat, covering the spot where my necklace lay hidden under my clothes.

"Don't ever do that again. Don't ever say that you did that. Never." My mind rushed back to hearing these same words from Mrs. DuVille. I better understood the incredible danger of speaking of un-Christian things.

Ann and Abigail let in a blustery wind as they entered the kitchen. I looked at them reprovingly.

Betty sat at the table. She looked pale.

"What is in your minds?" I scolded.

Betty trembled.

Ann turned on Mercy. "You told."

Betty gasped a few times, but she couldn't get air. She rose to her feet, but couldn't find equilibrium. She fell to the floor in a trembling fit.

I gathered the convulsing child into my arms.

Dr. Griggs came down the steep stairs. He carried a bowl of blood in his hands. He passed the bowl to me.

Goody Parris sat at the table, concern covering her blanched face, her fingers in a fury.

Abigail waited in a corner. "How's cousin Betty?"

Dr. Griggs came to where Goody Parris sat by the fire, covered in a blanket. "She seems well. I bled her, but I see nothing serious."

"We went to the shed," Abigail confessed.

"She may have taken a chill. I wouldn't concern yourself over much."

Goody Parris took Dr. Griggs's hands. "She's been distracted, forgetful of late. She's felt poorly for days. Is it like me? Has my illness spread to her?"

Dr. Griggs smiled warmly. "It's likely one of those childhood things. I doubt it will return. Not to worry."

I walked out with the doctor. I waved to him as he began his trek across the field.

I moved away from the house to dump the blood in the bowl against a tree. I looked toward the water pump and felt almost lured away. I was mesmerized at being alone in the night. I set the bowl on the ground. I removed my cap and let down my hair as I walked along a wooded path. I was at peace.

"Are you simple?" The Reverend Parris scolded. "Slaves never walk out alone at night. How many times have I told you this?" Instinctively, I raised my arms defensively. He grabbed me and pulled my face very close to his own. "And where is your cap?" He dragged me back toward the house.

As we entered, Abigail and Thomas startled and looked up. Abigail rose and took a step toward me, but I shook my head almost imperceptibly and she stopped where she was.

"Go to bed," The Reverend Parris yelled.

She ran from the room.

People of all ages trudged inside the meetinghouse. All looked somber and serious, dull and gray.

The Reverend Parris carried in Betty. Betty was listless and ill. I sat next to Thomas. Goody Parris sat next to me with Betty and held Betty's small hand. Betty fidgeted in her seat and I quietly scolded her. Mercy, Abigail, and Ann sat on the pew behind us.

Elizabeth Hubbard joined them. Elizabeth lived with her great aunt Rachel who was married to Dr. Griggs. While her aunt and uncle were persons of high standing in the community, like Mercy Lewis, Elizabeth had been taken in by the Griggs more as a servant than a niece.

Elizabeth was a slip of a girl with big, expressive eyes

who had a strong aspect of likeability about her. While Ann Putnam was open about her manipulation of her elders, Elizabeth could be canny and cunning, but I still felt there was a sweetness to be found buried beneath her surface.

"Let us offer prayers to the Lord God for our neighbors so that their hearts and minds may be strengthened," The Reverend Parris opened his Bible and read.

Rows of silent and still men, women, and children looked glazed as the reverend read to them from the Bible. I liked the Bible stories. They reminded me of the shaman's telling of our people's legends. I liked the man Jesus and his tribesmen. However, after the reading came the reverend's interpretation of the meaning of the stories. That part I didn't like.

Betty's fidgets turned into a thrashing squirm. She moved as if to run from the meetinghouse, but I held her back. I stilled her with a heavy arm across her shoulder. There would be a price to pay with the reverend later if I let Betty disrupt his service. He already cast an angry eye my way.

"Pray for Goody Good and her small daughter so that the demons that have rooted in her mind will not win her soul or that of the child."

We all answered. "Come among us, Emmanuel."

"Goody Osborne continues to feel poorly. Let us offer our prayers to God for the return of her health and spirit."

"Come among us, Emmanuel."

"My own daughter, Betty, has taken ill. I ask for your prayers for her return to health."

"Come among us, Emmanuel."

"Let us say together the Lord's prayer. Our father who art in heaven…"

Betty couldn't concentrate at prayer time and made a sound of distress that seemed rather like the barking of a dog.

Her body contorted in the most bizarre way.

The Reverend Parris stopped mid-prayer. "Betty, be still and reverent at all times in the house of the Lord."

Betty screamed wildly and hurled her Bible across the room. She sobbed while rubbing her arms and legs. Betty bolted from the meetinghouse.

Outside, Mercy, Abigail, Ann, and Elizabeth tried to appear casual as they drifted by a bench where the Reverend Parris, Goody Parris, and Dr. Griggs attempted to calm a hysterical Betty.

I pulled the girls away and sat them down to wait. I set down a basket of rye rolls to keep them occupied. Ann and Abigail both grabbed a roll, pulled it open and added a slice of cheese. They waited for me to walk away before they began to whisper.

Abigail said, "She says that something's crawling inside her."

"Like what?" Ann asked.

"Demons, I guess."

Mercy cut a slice of cheese and nibbled on it. "Do you think we called dark spirits?"

"No," Ann said. "I didn't really see anything in the egg. I made it up."

Mercy looked angry. "So you're not to marry William."

"Of course I am.

Mercy seemed disappointed that the egg and glass were false. "Do you think if we chanted or something it might be made to work?"

Abigail and Ann gave Mercy scornful looks.

"I want to know what my future holds," Mercy said. "I want to know if I will marry."

"You have nothing to offer, no family, no dowry," Ann

said. "Everyone knows you have no prospects."

Abigail nodded. "Truly, you're not likely to marry."

I moved closer to where the girls sat talking. "Be still. No more talk of that."

"But I want to know," Mercy said.

Mercy and Ann exited the woods at the edge of the Parris field at a full run. Sarah Good chased after them, tugging at Dorcas to keep up. Ann threw a roll from her basket at Dorcas before she dashed across the field. Dorcas stopped and picked up the roll. Goody Good didn't slow down.

Having watched this exchange from the loft window, I climbed down and swung open the door at the first pounding. Mercy and Ann ran inside panting. I began to close the door, but Goody Good pushed it open. She tottered, a little unsteady on her feet. "I'm hungry," she said without her usual forcefulness. "Dorcas, she's hungry. I need something to eat."

I had not seen Goody Good in person in some time. I was surprised to note the roundness of her midsection. Goody Good was with child. My guess was about four months gone. She was unsteady from the shifts in her body. She sat down heavily on the bench at the kitchen table.

Goody Parris called from the next room. "What is it, Tituba?" she asked me.

I held my finger to my lips to hush everyone. "Miss Ann and Miss Mercy have come to call," I responded.

Mercy spoke with Goody Parris in the next room. "Goody Putnam was concerned for Betty."

Ann pulled the basket from Mercy's arms as Goody Parris entered, leaning heavily on a stick. "Mother sent over some of her jams and breads."

I took the basket and set it on the table. I pulled a loaf of bread from the basket and cut off a slice. I handed it to

Goody Good. I poured her a cup of milk to help build her own milk.

"How thoughtful," Goody Parris said of Ann's basket. "Send her my thanks. Has Goody Sibley arrived yet with the herbs for my tea? She said she would come visiting today."

"Not yet." I pulled a cauldron from the fire and ladled two bowls full of stew.

The door opened and Dorcas entered, a bit of roll in her hand. She sat down next to her mother at the kitchen table and plowed into her bowl of stew.

"Abigail. Go outside and do your chores," Goody Parris ordered. "Take Mercy and Ann with you."

I whisked the girls out from underfoot. I knew Goody Parris wanted some quiet, but I also knew what she needed. "Shall I go see what holds up Goody Sibley with your herbs?"

Goody Parris nodded.

Soon, I was walking up to the Sibley home. Goody Sibley's spacious three-story home sported a wide porch on the front side. I had never been inside, but I had been told that the floors were all polished wood and all the windows had small squares of glass. She had many fine and beautiful things.

Goody Osborne sat in a chair on the porch covered in a blanket. She held her face to try to catch a ray of sun.

Goody Sibley struggled with an axe, attempting to split some logs for the fire. I admired that she had no slaves. She had a girl she paid to clean and cook and another girl took in her washing that she paid as well. These girls went to their home each night. She could afford a slave or servant, but opted not.

"Do you think you could do me a favor?" Goody Sibley asked.

Goody Osborne looked over.

Goody Sibley pointed in the direction of the parsonage.

"I promised Goody Parris some herbs for her pain. Can you carry them over to her?"

Goody Osborne struggled to stand with the help of a walking stick, a forty-nine year old woman with a sixty-nine year old's stick. "Stretching my legs will most likely do me good."

"No need," I said as I turned the corner around the side of Goody Sibley's house. Goody Sibley pulled a pouch from her pocket. She handed me the cloth. Inside was folded a weed that we had found eased Goody Parris's illness.

"Shall I stay a bit and help you?" I pointed to the wood she chopped.

"It's not likely Goody Parris will wish to wait, but if you happen to see John maybe you could ask him to help me with the firewood." She hired John's labor for difficult tasks from time to time, however, Mr. Parris took his earnings, unless he didn't know about it.

I smiled. "I'll keep an eye out."

The Reverend Parris and Dr. Griggs approached the house on horseback. I saw them coming and went out. The reverend would expect me to be on hand to take his horse after he dismounted.

As I passed near to the shed, I could hear Ann, Abigail, and Mercy.

Mercy said, "I think we should try a chant."

Abigail replied, "I don't know."

"How about this? Spirits come. Spirits come." Mercy rocked with her song.

Those silly girls were trying again at fortune telling. They understood little of the danger of acting as a shaman when you were not or, in this world, if you were.

Abigail clutched a handful of straw until her knuckles whitened. She screamed. She jumped up and ran to the corner of the shed to cower.

The Reverend Parris heard the screams and ran toward the sound with Dr. Griggs close behind him.

Ann attempted to calm Abigail, but she was too hysterical. Abigail flung her arms about in a defensive gesture.

"What is it, Abigail?" Ann asked.

"Didn't you see?"

"No. See what?" Mercy asked.

"A coffin. It looks like a coffin."

Ann and Mercy exchanged a look.

I reached the girls first, with the Reverend Parris quickly following. Abigail was running around the shed, yelling.

"Niece. What is this?" the Reverend Parris asked.

"Don't you see?"

Dr. Griggs rushed to Abigail, but he couldn't console her.

I glanced over to where the girls had been playing in the straw and saw the egg in the glass. I stood in front of the objects, using my skirts to block them from view, but the Reverend Parris saw and pushed me aside.

"Sorcery," he yelled. "We are a good Christian family. When will this community be rid of these pagan practices?"

"It's just a bit of cunning," Dr. Griggs ventured. It's a game to children."

"A game?"

"The girls are merely attempting to tell their fortunes by using the egg and glass."

"If these are the games they play, I will ensure that they have no time to play at all."

"You are too harsh."

Few others would dare to speak to the Reverend Parris in this way.

The Reverend Parris scowled at the doctor. "And why

did we suffer three thousand miles across stormy seas? Is it for us to bring these pagans, heathens, and savages to blessed salvation? There is only good and evil. You can be but one or the other."

In my raising, I was taught that there were as many ways to be as there were animals in the jungle. To my way of thinking, this was the Reverend Parris's problem. He thought that there was only one way. He did not see the struggle of the many spirits even in himself. He was one minute gentle with his children and nurturing with his ailing wife and in another minute angry, bitter, and hateful as the devil himself. He saw no diversity. You were Christian or no, Puritan or no, good or no, as if he would want all birds to be yellow.

He thought that evil was a fallen angel named Satan. Evil was a matter of perspective. To the ants on a stick, the monkey was evil, but when the jaguar had the monkey in its jaws, the jaguar was evil. Evil was your adversary, sometimes sent to test you. The Reverend Parris had lost touch with the natural world and listened to no spirit guide who could show him his way to defeat his adversaries.

16
Salem Village, February 1692

Betty and Abigail lay side by side in a soft bed, both thrashing and contorting their bodies. Betty turned her neck and back in a way that didn't seem possible. Abigail's mouth flopped open and she choked on the air she sucked in. I touched a cool cloth to Abigail's burning forehead.

The Reverend Parris sat next to Betty, holding down her shoulders, his face a portrait of fear and worry. He rested his hand on her stomach as if he could pull the pain from her. "Pray with me, Betty. Pray with me."

"It hurts like knives. Make it stop."

The Reverend Parris felt her comment like a rebuff. He looked away from her, struggling with the emotion showing on his face.

"Help me, Daddy."

I silently left the bedroom and went to the storage area where my family slept at night. I watched as John rolled out an elk fur on the floor in the crowded space.

Ahanu had given John this pelt. We keep it hidden under the shelves of the pantry. After our evening meal, we lay out our sleeping mat with the fur on top. John said that Ahanu and his wife slept between four furs, but we had only the one. It shielded us from the cold floor. We covered ourselves with our traveling cloaks and with a blanket I had made from rags. It was soft, warm, and comforting in a way that was hard to explain.

Violet went to bed easily and often slept through the night. She ran her hand over the fur and it sparked like stars in the night sky. This made her giggle. She lay down in the middle of the fur and sang a little song to herself as she soothed herself into first sleep.

I kissed her forehead.

"Sleep well, my little monkey."

"Do you think that monkey is Violet's spirit animal?" John asked.

John left questions of this nature to me more and more often. He didn't clearly remember the ways of our people. We spoke, acted, and lived so much as Christians.

"I was twelve years old when I was taken to Barbados. Same age as Abigail is today. Before that day…"

"What?"

"I remember everything."

John didn't know what to say. I saw the confusion on his face.

In a few hours, John and I awoke. John moved Violet to his other side. He kissed and stroked me until we were ready to be together. The three of us, flesh to flesh, on the warmth and comfort of our fur: these were my favorite moments.

"I wish I weren't lent out to Ingersoll," John said as he stroked my hair. "I wish I could be here with you and Violet during the daytime hours."

Violet curled into a tiny ball, two fingers in her mouth. "Daddy," she mumbled.

It crossed my mind that Violet didn't even speak the language of my people.

John rested a light hand on her that covered the whole of her chest and stomach. I had just witnessed this same gesture from the Reverend Parris and Betty. I wondered what John would do if Violet was pleading with him to help her. I believed that the reverend loved his daughter as much as John loved his.

Betty and Abigail only worsened. Dr. Griggs wrung his hands, unsure what to do. He called in a colleague from a nearby town. The Reverend Parris considered the condition of his family and asked several neighbors and ministers to consult with them at his house. I watched them gather from the loft window.

Along with the ministers known to him came a minister much revered among Puritans. The Reverend Cotton Mather had traveled the long distance from Boston.

The Reverend Mather wore the robes of the clergy as well as the white collar of his office; however he also sported the tallest white curls I had ever seen on a man. The ringlets brushed past his shoulders and he gave them a flip with his hand.

"The children are much tormented," the Reverend Parris told the gathering of men.

Dr. Griggs spelled out their symptoms. "Their stomachs roil and they hold down no food. They have pain, weakness and numbness. Most disturbing are the spasms and convulsions, often leading to loss of consciousness."

The Reverend Parris brought them two at a time to the loft to observe the behavior of the girls.

I had been making a tonic to encourage sleep, but he made me stop the day before the meeting so that the gentlemen could see all the full signs. When the last of the visitors went downstairs, I made a new draught to soothe the girls.

I could hear male voices speaking in hushed tones.

"Doctor, what is your opinion?"

"I admit to being at a loss. I've never seen such an ailment."

A voice I did not recognize asked, "What of the tea that your slave is brewing?"

"What? Tituba? She would never purposefully sicken

the children."

"Is this the slave from Barbados? Does she practice voodoo?"

"Of course not. I've never seen her act other than as a Christian woman."

"Slaves are adept at hiding their true nature."

There was a pause and a shuffling as one of the men arose from his chair. A thud on the table was followed by "I've brought you a book that I, myself, have written called *Memorable Providences*."

"That's most gracious of you, Rev. Mather," I heard the Reverend Parris respond. His voice held an element of respect and awe.

"I have seen this kind of thing before and have written of persons suffering at the hands of Satan. Read the story of the four Goodwin children who were similarly afflicted to your own children. A woman named Glover confessed to bewitching them and was hanged."

"Tituba has not bewitched my children," the Reverend Parris defended me but weakly and without conviction. He seemed to be pondering this idea that he had not considered previously.

"I will speak it since no one else dares. This illness is a commission of the devil. He has set loose his demons on the innocent. "

Another new voice intervened. "The truth of all things is not known to us. I recommend that we sit and wait on the providence of God to see what we might discover.

"Yes. Yes. Of course," the Reverend Parris said.

I took the tonic up to the girls. In the loft, I turned and stared out the attic window. I watched as Ann Putnam and Elizabeth Hubbard crossed the field in the distance. Elizabeth looked up and saw my silhouette in the upstairs window. She startled and jumped at the sight of me.

They split taking two directions. Ann walked in one direction toward her family's farm. Elizabeth walked in the opposite way toward Dr. Grigg's house where she lived.

John, alarmed by the talk in the house, had followed me. He came and stood behind me at the window.

"We must do something to help," I said. "They seem so ignorant of the spirit world."

I watched Elizabeth as she continued across the field alone in the dark. Her eyes darted nervously behind each tree she passed. She shook and grasped at her throat. She screeched an inhuman sound.

"Something's wrong." I ran down the stairs and out the door. John followed.

Elizabeth howled and took off running at full speed. She kicked and turned in a bizarre dance. As she jumped a small brook, she scooped up a stone on the opposite shore and chucked it at something unseen. Elizabeth attempted to jump to the low branch of a tree, but she did not make it and fell.

I raced across the field. I hadn't been aware of Dr. Griggs. He reached his niece just before I did. He pulled Elizabeth from the tree, her struggling in his arms all the time. Elizabeth thrashed on the ground, slashing at an invisible foe. Dr. Griggs tried to pull her into his arms, but she pummeled his chest and scratched at his face.

"What is this?" he begged.

"Wolves," she whispered, with just barely enough breath to answer.

Dr. Griggs looked around. "I don't see any wolves."

John and I exchanged a look. He shrugged. John waved his arms and yelled, "Be gone wolves. Out of here."

"Yellow eyes in the darkness." Elizabeth was still hysterical, but she was calming. "Three. They were nipping at my heels. Huge wolves."

"There are no wolves." Dr. Griggs picked up the flailing girl, but it was clear she did not care for logic. "John has chased them away."

Dr. Griggs glanced at John and so John did his wolf dance again. "Be gone," he yelled.

"He hasn't."

"You're safe now." Dr. Griggs carried her toward their home, half comforting her and half restraining her.

John and I stood and watched them disappear into the woods. We stood in the fading light of day, breathing heavily. We realized both at once that we were not alone.

The Reverend Parris's guests witnessed all. We stood under the clouds as they crossed in front of the rising moon. I shivered from the cold. Many words unspoken, we turned and walked back to the Parris house.

We crossed the threshold of the front door and slipped into our storage room. We could hear the Reverend Parris making his farewell remarks to his guests.

I went into the kitchen to see if the family wanted their evening meal. They did not.

I returned to the storage closet and we stayed there until the house grew still, quiet, and dark. I crawled into John's arms on his side of the sleeping mat. He covered both Violet and me with the rag blanket. He kissed my forehead.

"I can't watch that little girl being eaten up," I said.

He pulled me closer. "There must be a shape-shifter come to cause this sickness."

"The Taino shaman said that the master is a kenaimas, hairy with bushy eyebrows and knobby knees who shifts into a dog."

"A dog is like a wolf? We must be wary. Hold tight to your zemi."

My hand went to my necklace. "Yes. It's strong protection."

John kissed me and fell into his first sleep, but I lay awake lost in thought. When the house was still, I got up and crept quietly up the ladder into the loft.

The Reverend Parris stood in the children's bedroom. He looked stricken and tears flowed down his cheeks. He saw me and dried his eyes.

"What are you doing?" he lashed out.

"I wanted to check on the children."

The Reverend Parris lowered his head and slunk away.

I stood stone still for a long time. When the house was again at peace and I was sure that the Reverend Parris had gone to sleep, I sat on Betty's bed. Betty tossed and turned. I rested my hand on her shoulder and she woke up.

"I have something for you," I said. "Something to wear."

I took off my necklace and put it around Betty's neck. I covered it with Betty's nightclothes. "It will protect you. Keep you safe, but you must never let anyone see it." I rocked Betty until she relaxed in my arms. "It's important. Do you understand?"

Betty nodded that she did.

I looked at Abigail who fretted in her sleep.

"What do you dream, little girl?" I asked her. I kissed her head. "I wish I had one for you too." My hand rested at my throat filling the emptiness there. "Stay close to Betty and her protection may shower on you as well."

I climbed down from the sleeping loft. I found the Reverend Parris in the kitchen. He sat near the fire reading a book, I presumed the tome left by the Reverend Mather.

I felt the grip of fear as I departed the room.

The people of Salem Village entered the meetinghouse. The Reverend Parris stood at the door. He held two books in his arms, one in addition to his normal Bible. He wore black robes and a white cravat around his neck signaling the dignity of his office.

His red-rimmed eyes indicated several sleepless nights, nights he had spent buried in his two books. He glared at his neighbors as they entered the church. He looked as tormented as the girls.

Dr. Griggs pulled him to one side. "I now believe an evil hand is on the girls." Dr. Griggs said.

"What brings you to this conclusion?"

"Elizabeth…"

"Same as the others?"

Dr. Griggs nodded.

The Reverend Parris patted the doctor's arm.

"This is a legal matter, not a medical one," Dr. Griggs said. "I'll call a meeting of the village selectman at Ingersoll's after services."

The Reverend Parris nodded, turned and walked into the church. He took his place at the front. He turned his thoughts inside. He skimmed his Bible until he abruptly slammed it shut. He raised his hands indicating that the congregation should stand.

"We live bordered by a wilderness that is the domain of the devil. We struggle daily to maintain our foothold. It must be supposed that Satan is exceedingly disturbed by our inroads and has a plan to gain back his domain. We now see his plan come to fruition. Let us offer prayers to the Lord God so that we may be saved from the evil that has infested our village."

The congregation looked at each other, catching one another's eyes. These people were brothers and sisters, husbands, wives and children. Of the little over five hundred occupants, almost all were related in some way.

"As you know my daughter and my niece have been ill these past weeks. I ask for your prayers."

"Come among us, Emmanuel," the congregation said sincerely in response.

"Now a third of our children is touched, Dr. Griggs's ward Elizabeth Hubbard. These children need our tender care and…"

The congregation gasped. This news of Elizabeth was a surprise.

"I ask you to cast out the malevolent forces among us with your words. You must repent your own evil acts as we pray for the afflicted children. I call for a fasting day for each of us to repent our collective sins."

Goody Sibley leaned close to Goody Nurse and whispered, "Those poor girls."

Goody Nurse nodded and repeated what she had just heard, likely all she had heard, "Poor girls."

The Reverend Parris held the congregation in their seats all through the day and until the sun set outside the window. Some people fell asleep. Those who stayed awake became listless. I thought they were probably also angry, but this they did not openly show.

The Reverend Parris stood firm at the pulpit his eyes on John and I. I sat wide awake, rigid, and returned his gaze.

Mr. Putnam leaned over and spoke a few words to Dr. Griggs. The Reverend Parris's eyes flew over the congregation and landed hard on the offending duo. He need not speak a word.

This went on until late in the night.

17
Salem Village, February 1692

The sun was barely showing in the sky when a knocking came at the door. I opened it to a blast in the face of cold wind and snow. Goody Good and Dorcas stood outside.

I looked toward the edge of the property. Curiously, Goody Sibley trudged across the field toward the parsonage with a dog on a rope. She tied the dog to a rail, stood and watched.

"She doesn't want to come over here," Goody Good said, "but I'm not afraid to come in and warm up by the fire for a bit."

"I'll get you some cheese." I waved over Goody Sibley.

Goody Good took the cheese I offered and cut a thick slice of bread from a loaf for herself. She pulled out some of the soft middle of the bread and handed it to Dorcas. Dorcas lay on the floor in front of the fire and Goody Good cozied into the reverend's chair. They both fell into a deep sleep. I noted the progress of Goody Good's pregnancy as I lay a blanket across her lap.

In a minute, Goody Sibley knocked and entered the Parris kitchen. "Reverend Parris?"

"He's gone to Boston to consult about Betty's sickness," John answered.

Goody Sibley peeked into the front room. She saw Goody Parris on her bed, Goody Good in the big chair and Dorcas on the floor—all asleep. Goody Sibley listened to the sound of their breathing in concert.

"Excellent. I wished to speak to you both alone." She sat at the kitchen table next to John. She leaned in and spoke in a low voice. "You're in danger. People are speaking warily of you. You are an unknown, different from them."

"But I have lived in the village for three years. They know me."

"I know you. I know you are a good person. They do not. What we need to do is reveal who is responsible for the illness so that we can make them undo the spell on the children. That will take their eyes off you."

"I want to help ease the girl's suffering," I said.

"We'll make a witchcake," Goody Sibley said.

"I'm concerned about the rye," I said. "It was unclean when I thrashed it. I keep Violet away from the barn, but the other girls play in the tainted straw almost daily. That's where they were when their woes first began."

"This illness does mimic the effects of some plants," Goody Sibley said. "There is a yellow flower called an Angel's Trumpet. A little in your tea gives you interesting visions, but too much can be deadly."

I sent John to the lean-to to gather some of the straw and he did. "Look for the ones with little kernels on them," I instructed him.

Goody Sibley nibbled on a bit of rye straw with no noticeable effect. "No," she said. "We all eat the rye. If it had gone awry, its impact would be more widespread. Don't you think?"

I was taken aback by being asked my opinion. "Yes. I agree that makes sense."

"This witchcake. How's it done?" John asked.

"It's made of rye meal and the urine of one of the afflicted girls. Then it's baked in ashes and fed to a dog. The dog is bewitched by the cake, becomes a familiar, and will point out the witch."

"I'm not sure this is a good idea," John said. He looked to me. "It riles the evil spirits."

I turned to Goody Sibley. "This is how it's done with your people? This is the usual way?"

"Oh yes," Goody Sibley assured me.

Goody Good had roused from slumber and was listening in. She gave a vile laugh.

"What do you need?" I asked.

Goody Sibley smiled. "I need a little of the girl's morning urine." This explained her early morning call. She wished to be on hand before morning chores were completed and the girl's piss pot was emptied.

We sent Goody Good and Dorcas on their way before we made the cake and put it into the fire. Goody Sibley sniffed and scrunched up her nose.

Goody Parris, groggy even at first light, her eyes heavy with sleep, stirred in her slumber. "What's that smell?" she called.

"I burned a bit of toast for my breakfast. I'm sorry, Ma'am."

I opened the door to let in some fresh air and saw that Mercy Lewis stood there. Mercy entered the kitchen and took in the scene. She looked at the rye flour dusting the table and the empty piss pot to the side. She glanced back at the dog. At first, she couldn't make sense of it, but then enlightenment came.

"You made a witchcake."

Goody Sibley rushed to shush her.

"I thought you said this was the usual way."

Mercy snickered. "It is if you're a cunning woman."

I was horrified.

Curiosity took over Mercy. "What's it show?" she asked. "Who's the witch?"

Goody Sibley took the hot cake, careful of her fingers, and crumbled it into a bowl. She blew on it a bit and then added a touch of milk on top. I untied the dog as Goody Sibley set the bowl of cake down on the porch.

We all watched, holding our breath, sucking in the tension. The dog ate the cake, sniffed around a bit for more and then circled three times and lay down on the sunniest spot on the porch. The dog shut his eyes and went to sleep.

"What's it mean?"

We all looked bewildered.

I walked through the sunny, frigid commons toward Ingersoll's tavern where John was working. I'd brought him his midday meal. Goody Parris had sent along Ann Putnam to keep an eye on me. I knew this was more because Ann was wearing thin Goody Parris's nerves. She trusted me to make my destination.

William Porter crossed the commons along with his father, Joseph Porter, and his uncle, Israel Porter. This was unusual and so all eyes followed their progress. Beyond the Sunday midday meal, the Porters didn't often visit the village, preferring to go into Salem Town for business and shopping.

Ann saw William and fell into step behind him. I laughed at William's obvious discomfort. Mr. Joseph Porter shared my smile with me.

As Mr. Joseph Porter and William reached the door to Ingersoll's tavern, Ann attempted to follow William inside. Mr. Porter put out a hand to stop her.

"Not this time, young lady," he said. "This is a meeting for adults."

"But I'm twelve," she said. She kicked some dirt and sulked.

He passed me through and then the door slammed

against Ann's protests.

Inside, most of the village's selectmen were crowded around a table. Many had a pint in front of them. I glanced around, but the Reverend Parris did not seem to be present. The Porters sat in the rear of the room.

"Welcome Joseph, Israel," Mr. Higginson, a man I did not know well said. "It's been a long time since you've attended a village committee meeting." He nodded to William.

"What do we speak of this morning?" Mr. Israel Porter asked.

Mr. Ingersoll looked at me and said, "John is out back." He waited a moment for me to move toward the tavern's rear door.

From the back door threshold, I saw John stacking logs against the exterior wall of a shed. He picked up an armload of wood to haul into the tavern. As I held open the door, I saw Mr. Thomas Putnam stand to speak and I heard his reply to Mr. Israel Porter.

"I regret that we must discuss the behavior of the Reverend Parris of late." Mr. Higginson said.

"Are you prepared to admit that he is not who you want as our spiritual leader?" Mr. Israel Porter asked.

"These are unusual times," Mr. Putnam admitted.

Ann crept around the building. She attempted to catch a look at William through the windows. She pushed past me in the rear threshold into the tavern and crouched down behind the bar. When Mr. Ingersoll saw her, he winked. Ann smiled in return. Mr. Ingersoll handed Ann a cup of water and a bit of rye. She nibbled as she stared at William.

"Parris is greedy. First, he held us up for more than a year with preposterous contract negotiations. And, then, the conveyance of the parsonage to himself was fraudulent," Mr. Porter said. "And his constant harassment about his fee…"

"Not this." Dr. Griggs appeared disturbed. "I wish to talk of the three girls."

Ann choked on the bit of bread. She grasped her throat and struggled for air.

"Thomas! William!" Mr. Ingersoll called.

Mr. Putnam came to her in time to see his daughter vomit and fall into convulsions. He looked incredulous, disbelieving.

The Parris girls lay in their beds. Betty ran her hands up and down her twitching and contorting arms. Abigail choked as if she couldn't catch a breath. I tried to calm the girls' hysterical fits, but without success.

"Hands. Invisible hands," Abigail whined. She said this though no one was near her, touching her.

I was at a loss for what to do.

The Reverend Parris stood behind me in the doorway, building a seething anger.

At Dr. Griggs's house, Elizabeth Hubbard cowered away from visions of apparitions. In her eye, a shadow flew into the second-story window of the Griggs house into her bedroom. The shadow crept toward Elizabeth and filled the space with its presence. The shadow took the shape of a dark-skinned woman who pricked at Elizabeth with a knife. Elizabeth screamed.

Dr. Griggs ran into Elizabeth's room.

"Ghost. She has a knife. Watch your back."

To Elizabeth, the apparition raised the knife and brought it down between her uncle's shoulder blades.

From Dr. Griggs's point of view, hers were ghosts only she could see.

In the Putnam home, Ann vomited into a bowl that Mercy held for her. Ann's mother was more hysterical than Ann. Mercy was horrified.

The next Sunday, the Reverend Parris stood at his pulpit. His appearance was more disheveled than even the previous week.

The congregation was silent, fearful, except for the four girls who moaned and contorted, drawing uncomfortable eyes from those people who were around them.

I held my breath.

The Reverend Parris began. "I've invited our neighboring ministers for a day of prayer." He indicated several religious men. "These learned men initially advised me to sit still and wait upon the providence of God."

I let out my breath. He seemed calm and reasonable enough on this day.

"But, more than a month has passed since these afflictions began. It sweeps plague-like through our village."

Elizabeth screamed.

The Reverend Parris looked at the girls. "Their bodies assume strange postures as if bitten by invisible agents. They turn this way and that."

Betty moaned and cried.

"We all," he indicated the ministers, "agree that the sickness is the work of the devil."

Ann ran out of the meetinghouse.

"Tituba," the Reverend Parris called me out. "Gather the girls and take them to Ingersoll's. Wait for our prayers to end. We will question them."

I picked up Betty and guided Elizabeth and Abigail out the door. Mr. Putnam ran after me. Dr. Griggs followed. Mercy Lewis came after that. Another half dozen people stood up.

"Sit!" the Reverend Parris insisted. "This is not an amusement for your entertainment."

Several people returned to their seats.

For this meeting at Ingersoll's, all the senior village men were there, including the Reverend Parris. I wrangled the four girls as John tended the fire. Mercy hid in the shadows at the back of the room.

A dozen men gathered around a nervous Ann who sat in a chair in the middle of the room. She looked pale and wretched.

"Ann, then what happened?" Mr. Putnam continued his examination of his daughter.

"We went out to the barn. Abigail showed us how to drop an egg into the glass."

Mr. Putnam's eyes landed on me accusingly. "And who showed Abigail this magic?"

William stared, enthralled with Ann's story. Mercy watched Ann getting all of William's attention. She was annoyed.

Mr. Putnam jumped to his feet. "Does Tituba tell stories of Barbados? Of voodoo?"

"Yes. She tells us of Barbados."

The Reverend Parris sucked in a raspy breath. He was taken aback by this acknowledgment that I told stories. I had always been careful to only tell them outside of the Reverend Parris's earshot.

Abigail hurdled herself toward the fireplace, attempting to go up the chimney. "I want to burn," she screamed.

Dr. Griggs jumped to his feet just as I grabbed Abigail, within inches of the blaze. The flames licked her sleeve alighting the cloth. I put it out by clapping it with my skirt as John joined me in holding her back. Dr. Griggs took hold of Abigail and examined her wound.

Ann hid in the corner. She dramatically shook and cried. William laid his hands upon Ann's shoulders and Ann grasped his neck. They looked intimate.

Mercy couldn't stand this. She ran to William. "I know something," she shouted, her voice much louder than needed.

All eyes turned to Mercy and the room quieted. There was an intake of breath as everyone waited.

Mercy pointed an accusing finger at me. "She made a witchcake."

18
Salem Village, February 1692

Betty sat at the kitchen table. It had been weeks since she had been out of her bed. I'd brought her soups and teas, but no rye. I made meal out of maize and cake from that. Her health had improved a good bit giving credence to my theory about the involvement of the fungus on the rye in her illness. But, since she had risen, it had been hard to keep her from the rye. They paid the minister in rye and the reverend insisted that I bake it.

Violet banged two wooden spoons together until she got bored. She shakily stood and pulled herself up using the edge of the table. Her eyes followed me as I worked.

Betty pulled a hunk off the rye loaf on the table. She offered it to Violet. Violet took it and brought it to her mouth. I slapped it out of her hand. Betty picked it up from the floor and nibbled. I pulled it from her hand as well.

"Leave her be," the Reverend Parris bellowed. "She's hungry. She needs some bulk."

Just like she needs to be bled again, I thought. Little wonder the girls were slow to recover.

Violet crawled to a corner under the kitchen table. Violet was smart and curious. Soon, I would not be able to shield her from the world into which she was born. She already knew to be silent and out of the way when the Reverend Parris was in the room. In the house, Betty or Goody Parris would play with her on occasion, but otherwise everyone else ignored her. Violet was figuring out that she was not part of this community.

"The rye bread is not good for Betty's recovery," I informed him helpfully.

Betty took a small bite and grinned. As I reached for it, the Reverend Parris picked up a nearby pot and slammed my hand. My fingers pounded as I tested them to ensure that they continued to function.

The house had been tense since the reverend discovered that I had performed an occult practice under his roof. It didn't matter that I knew nothing of pagans. When asked, I could have spoken of Goody Sibley, but her heart was good and she was my friend. In additon to this, she was a wealthy, respected gentlewoman while I was a slave. It was likely that the selectmen knew of her involvement already and opted not to know it. I could see no value in speaking her name.

Betty grabbed at her throat and fell to the floor in convulsions. She gasped in an attempt to breathe. I ran to her, but the Reverend Parris pushed me out of the way. The Reverend Parris loosed Betty's shift at the neck and saw my necklace at Betty's throat. He yanked the necklace from around Betty's neck. In one fluid motion, he rose while at the same time backhanding me.

"What have you done to my girl?"

His face twisted in rage. He grabbed a broom and struck me in the neck with its handle. I tasted the tang of blood as it flooded my mouth.

"You've bewitched my children and brought evil forces into my house." He shook the necklace in his clutched hand.

"It's for protect…" I couldn't get out my explanation before he hit my back with the broom. Bile filled my throat and I swallowed it down along with my cry of alarm. My head swam, but the pain of the stick in the same place on my back brought me back.

"You lure the children to you and away from their families. You pull them from their parents' loving breasts with ill intent. You will confess to this magic. "

Parris cast the broom aside and threw me like the twig doll onto a chair. "You will tell them you're a witch. Only confession and penitence can save your soul."

"But, I'm not a witch, " I protested.

"You give all appearances of the converted, but I suspect that you truly are not. This is not the influence of the devil on the innocent. You are the devil's own. I should cut off your head."

"No."

He shook me hard until my teeth chattered and he was exhausted by the effort.

"Stop," I said.

"Say you're a witch. Say it."

He threw my necklace, retrieved from Betty's throat, into the fire. I made a grab for it, but he kicked it away.

"Is this pretty little thing what you want?"

He paced the room, gathering his anger. He moved in close to me. He grabbed me by my shoulders and captured my eyes with his sinister ones. His voice was low and he appeared to be thinking, but his words were menacing. I struggled to release myself from his grasp.

"You will say what I know is true or I will sell Violet. You know what I mean. I will sell her and let her be raised as a whore. You will never see her again. You will not have her to love."

He punched me to the floor and kicked me in the torso.

John strode into the kitchen with a load of firewood, just as I cried out. John's eyes turned mean and cold. He dropped the wood, all save one sturdy limb.

"What is this?" he asked.

The Reverend Parris stood over my inert body breathing heavily.

John rushed at the Reverend Parris with the limb.

"John. No, John."

The two men came at each other. The Reverend Parris, no fighter, picked up a chair and poked at John with its legs.

I knew John would kill him, so I threw my arms around his waist and held fast. I enveloped him and protected him with my body against the Reverend Parris.

John tried to push me aside, but I held on. It was when John saw that I was getting the worst of it that he finally stopped.

It was only then that I noticed the din in the room. Violet cowered in the corner screaming. Betty was also yelling out to her father. It was when he heard this that he also stopped. He tried to regain his power.

"Say you've bewitched my children. Say you're a witch."

He was correct that it had been many years that I had been pretending to be someone that I was not. I saw this as no different.

"I'm a witch," I said.

The Reverend Parris picked up Betty and took her from the room.

A monster, hairy and knobby kneed, wielded a broomstick. I tried to wrestle it from him, but he would not release it. I whirled, turned into a yellow bird and flew out from the window.

I awoke from a nightmare. John tended my wounds. He rocked and hummed as he did.

The door to our space was open, so I could hear the Reverend Parris loudly interrogating Abigail in her bedroom.

"Someone did torture me," Abigail said.

"Was it Tituba?"

"I don't know. Someone was pricking me."

"I've written it all down for you. You understand. You must sign this legal deposition before I can help you."

"A deposition? What is it?"

"It's a true accounting of all that has happened. All the selectman wish to end this. Your friend Ann has signed. Elizabeth will as well."

"I don't want to get Tituba into trouble."

"This is what's best for everyone."

There was silence and John and I both imagined Abigail doing as she must, doing what her father has demanded her to do.

The first rays of sun peeked at the window. Time seemed to have lost all meaning. It was still mostly dark, but soon would be a new day.

"We'll go tonight," John said.

John believed that, if we ran from this life, the People of the Dawn would help us. John and I had discussed this many times, but I was afraid and would not go. On this day, he did not need to ask. We both knew that we would run. It was time to go.

I pulled the rag blanket up to my chin.

"I must work at Ingersoll's today. Will you be all right?"

I kissed John long, but lightly with my swollen lips.

"I will be now."

John and I rose. We walked through the storeroom, picking various items to take with us, mostly food, and put them in the covered basket I had made for Violet. We rolled our mats with our fur and hid them with the basket of food.

John left for his day of work and I went into the kitchen

to make Goody Parris's breakfast. I poked a stick at the embers of the fire. I searched through the ashes, but I couldn't find my zemi. My protection was gone.

Finally, I swung the kettle out of the fire and poured hot water into the teapot to steep. I went into the parlor and propped the pillows for Goody Parris and then I went back to the kitchen for the tea. I returned and handed her a cup. I set the tray beside her bed.

She caught my hand and pulled me down to sit on the bed at her side. "Thank you, Tituba," she said. "For all you've done for my family. You've been a godsend."

"So all eyes have turned to me?"

"Elizabeth said that Goody Good followed her in the shape of a giant wolf."

"And me? What did she say of me?"

"She says you flew down to her and pinched her." Ann named you and Goody Osborne as witches." Goody Parris lowered her eyes.

"That doesn't make any sense."

"They plan to hang you," Goody Parris said.

I jumped as a pounding began at the door. I looked warily toward it. The knocking came harder. Goody Parris and I stared at the wooden barrier.

"Constable Herrick here. Open. In the King's name, open the door!"

Still I could not move toward the door. My forehead broke out in a sweat and I began to tremble.

Violet's little head peeked around the corner. At a gesture from me, she toddled to my side and clutched at my skirt. She felt my tension but knew better than to cry out. I lifted her to sit on the bed beside me.

Constable Herrick pushed open the door and entered uninvited. He was a man in his middle years. His face was without emotion, but his militia uniform sent shivers through me.

I held Violet's head closer to my chest and felt her arms come around my neck.

Constable Herrick nodded to Goody Parris. "Sorry to disturb your morning, Ma'am."

"Constable. What can I do for you?"

My eyes darted, looking for a way out. Goody Parris gripped my hand and held it all the tighter.

"Is the reverend about?"

"Not at present."

"The yeomen of the village have sworn a complaint stating that Tituba and two others used the occult to injure four girls. It's a capital offense to invoke evil spirits." He held up a parchment. "I have a warrant. I must apprehend her."

"Tituba only?" Goody Parris asked.

"The warrant covers Sarah Osborne and Sarah Good as well."

Goody Parris shook her head in sadness.

Constable Herrick let in another officer who began a search of the house. The constable stayed close to me.

"Where does Tituba sleep?" the constable asked.

Goody Parris directed with her eyes. "The storage room."

The second constable went up the stairs to continue his search. I could hear the whimpers of Betty and Abigail in their beds.

"What does the warrant charge?" Goody Parris asked. These were questions that I would not have thought to ask.

"Suspicion of witchcraft. It claims that she did injury to Elizabeth Parris, Abigail Williams, Ann Putnam, and Elizabeth Hubert of Salem Village."

"What injury?"

"It does not specify."

"The girls are here in their beds. They are sick, but not injured."

The constable made no answer.

"Where will you take her?"

"She'll spend the night in Ipswich," Constable Herrick said. "There's to be a hearing at Ingersoll's tomorrow at 10:00 am."

I stood, picked up Violet, and held her close, tight in my arms. She nuzzled her face into my neck and softly cried. I wanted to give her my mother's zemi, but it was gone. I wanted to give her something to remember me by, but I had nothing.

"You're a sweet girl," I said. "Always remember that I love you." I whispered in a slight hiss into her ear, "And remember, wherever you go, whomever you are with, that you are mine."

I leaned down and kissed Goody Parris's cheek.

Into my ear, she whispered, "I'll watch out for Violet. When the girls are better, they will help. God bless you and keep you, Tituba."

Upstairs, I could hear Betty wail. "Say goodbye to them for me." I handed Violet into Goody Parris's arms, but she would not release. She held tight to my neck. When I pulled her loose, she screamed. She began to yowl like a hurt cub.

Constable Herrick pulled us apart and hustled me out the door.

The other militiaman waited in a buckboard. Constable Herrick took hold of my arm before we reached the wagon. Out of earshot, he asked, "What happened to your face?"

I didn't bother to answer.

19
Salem Village, March 1692

The whole town waited in Ingersoll's Tavern. Some town folk had packed a lunch basket of johnnycake and ale. They came prepared for a day's amusement. Other people came prepared for something else. They carried rocks, sticks or guns.

The buckboard approached the tavern from Ipswich where we had been held the night in a pigsty whose floor was covered with infected grain. The buckboard carried Goody Osborne, Goody Good, and me.

As I stepped down from the wagon, a bright yellow warbler flew close to my head. I wondered what this bird sought to tell me. My head felt woozy and I wondered for a moment if the yellow bird was even real. I watched the path of its darting flight for a moment.

Goody Ann Putnam, Ann's mother, rushed to the front of the crowd. Her face was flushed and her hands twisted. "Die witches!" she yelled. "Burn in hell." Others joined her angry jeers.

These were people I had known over the last several years. I had brought Goody Putnam herbs when she felt ill. I'd baked her stews. I plowed and tilled the Putnam fields. I went to the same church as most of those people. I served them a midday meal every Sunday. I made blankets they used to cover their bodies when cold. I made soap that kept them clean. I made them baskets they used to carry all sorts of items. All this went out the window when they feared for their children.

The yellow bird flew in front of my eyes, recalling my attention to her.

The constables held back the crowd as they escorted us into Ingersoll's. The inside was packed and people overflowed from the tavern into the common. It was a loud, stinking chaos of humanity.

I searched frantically among the faces for John. When I saw him, I tried to run into his arms, but the constable held me back.

John rushed to me, held me as if he wouldn't let me go. I saw the constable watching us, keeping a wary eye. He seemed to think better of trying to separate us.

"Take Violet and you go without me," I whispered into John's ear.

"No. Never. We'll all go together. In a few days you'll be home and…."

"He'll never forgive me or you." He knew I was speaking of the Reverend Parris. "I'm asking you to save Violet while you can."

"You may come along, John." Constable Herrick grabbed me and pulled me toward the door. "This is bedlam. We must move to a larger space. We cannot proceed in such turmoil. We're moving the proceedings to the meetinghouse."

"You can't save me," I whispered into John's ear as the constable pulled me from his arms. "You can only save Violet."

It was calmer at the Salem Village Meetinghouse—still crowded, but with mostly just the principals. The rest had been forced to remain outside.

A table at the front of the room served as the dock. Sitting next to the dock were the four girls: Betty and Abigail from the Parris household, along with Ann Putnam and Elizabeth Hubbard. It was surprising that the girls were there. That was unusual.

I nodded to Betty and she smiled, but she didn't look good. Ann jabbed her with a pointy finger on a twisted hand that reminded me of her mother. None of the girls could focus their eyes. They looked pale and afraid. Elizabeth scratched until she drew blood from her arms. I wanted to comfort them, but I knew that I could not.

I was made to wait in the vestibule with Goody Good and Goody Osborne. Constable Herrick and his men stayed close at hand. This was meant to separate us from the proceedings, but the church was too small to be effective at this.

"All rise."

Two magistrates entered the wide doors of the meetinghouse. The first stomped down the center aisle. He was stern and imposing. This I assumed to be John Hathorne who, I was told, was to be one of two judges that would preside over the initial hearings.

Jonathan Corwin of neighboring Salem Town followed. Judge Corwin was a fancy merchant and politician known to many here in Salem Village. He had a reputation as a fair man however he could be easily swayed by public opinion.

The Reverend Mather, who wore his tall white wig followed. He took a seat in a middle pew.

The Reverend Parris trailed in behind them. He looked smug and self-satisfied as he passed me by, haughty as he walked down the aisle and wrathful as he stood behind the judges. It was clear to anyone who cared to look that he had made up his mind as to the outcome before the beginning of these proceedings.

Judge Hathorne turned to the Reverend Parris. Judge Hathorne spoke in a commanding voice that carried across the teeming room. "Reverend. Lead us in prayer."

The Reverend Parris raised his hands to the heavens.

His voice boomed like thunder. His words went on and on and I lost interest until I heard the words "The devil is loosed in Salem," but I could not hear the rest of his words for the pounding of my own heart in my ears.

Judge Hathorne introduced Mr. Ezekiel Cheever who would be writing things down and then he had Constable Herrick read out the charges; "Suspicion of witchcraft."

After the reading of the charges, the Reverend Parris took a seat at the table beside Mr. Cheever. He took out his own quill and paper, clearly of a mind to make his own account of the events at hand.

The judge turned his eyes on me and studied the bluing of day old bruises. He said, "Understand that witchcraft is a capital offense. Some crimes are considered so heinous that, if found guilty, you may pay for your crimes with your life. This is one. This is a death penalty crime."

I tried to swallow and found I could not. A shining broke out on my forehead. I understood that in minutes I would be forced to make a choice for my own life or for Violet's and John's. I knew without doubt that the Reverend Parris would make good on his threats.

"Constable, did you search the possessions of the accused?

"I did, your honor. No incriminating artifacts were found."

"And do they attend church?"

"Tituba is most regular. The other two are known to miss services. Goody Good has not attended in years."

Betty moaned in pain and Abigail screamed out in response.

"Very well Constable." Judge Hathorne was disconcerted. He examined the girls for a minute. He shuffled through his papers. He brought his eyes level with the crowded room and calmed his demeanor.

"This is a preliminary inquiry," he began, "to investigate these very serious charges. From the results, we will determine if indictments are warranted and, if issued, there will be a trial by a jury of freeholders of Essex County. " His eyes traveled over the crowd for a full minute. "Sarah Good. Come forward."

Abigail screamed for a second time. The crowd could not contain their comments about the commotion.

Constable Herrick walked Goody Good from the vestibule to the dock.

Goody Good looked more wild than usual. She ranted and struggled against the constable. Dorcas ran down the aisle after her. A couple of people made taunts into their hands so that their lips could not be identified.

"Sarah Good, wife of laborer William Good of Salem Village," Constable Herrick declared before he retreated.

Judge Hawthorn rose. He stood over Sarah Good, close into her own space, his jutting stomach nearly touching her six-months-pregnant one. His voice was louder than it need be. "Sarah Good, have you made a contract with the devil?"

She looked attacked, stunned by the tone of this question. "No."

"Why do you hurt these children?"

She looked down at her soon-to-be babe. "I don't hurt them," she defended.

Judge Hathorne looked to the girls, who fidgeted and squirmed in their seats. They looked sickly and uncomfortable. Elizabeth's legs seemed to be drawn up into knots and she slapped at them.

"Look at her," Judge Hathorne pointed a sharp finger at Goody Good as he instructed the girls. "See if this is the person who hurts you."

Ann pointed her shaky, crooked finger, a silent

accusation.

"She's pinching me now," whined Elizabeth. Any fool could see that she was not fully aware of anything beyond her own pain.

The crowd erupted again in remarks and jeers. The noise was daunting.

"I don't torment them," Goody Good protested, screaming over the din in the room.

Someone from the pews threw something at Goody Good. I could not see what. She ducked and flinched.

"Who then?"

"I don't know. Someone else. You brought in two others."

It was at this inopportune moment that Goody Osborne coughed. Goody Good looked toward her.

The Reverend Parris leaned toward Mr. Cheever. He nodded toward Goody Osborne and Mr. Cheever made a note.

Constable Herrick held up Goody Osborne. Goody Osborne looked lost and confused. With her own poor health, she was in a fog, unsure of what was befalling her.

The Reverend Parris abandoned his scribbles and moved next to me in the vestibule. He whispered into my ear. "I know a man who travels into the far wilderness to the north. Snow falls deeper than my house is tall."

I startled. I wanted to be brave, but I could not control my shaking.

"His wife is sad at the loss of their two-year-old son. The wilderness man thinks another toddler would cheer her." He pressed his thumb into a spot on my upper arm we both knew to be deeply purple.

I struggled to calm my breath. I pulled back my shoulders and glared at him.

He smiled, leered at me with the snarl of a dog.

The yellow bird frantically pecked at the triangular windows of the meetinghouse with its tiny beak.

"I believe you to be a man of your word," I said. I waited a moment for sanity to come back to him. "If I say the words you wish, do you promise that no harm will come to John or Violet?"

He considered and then he nodded.

I wasn't convinced that a nod was sufficient to bind him.

"Say it," I insisted.

He smiled with only half his mouth, an ugly, sly grimace. "I give you my word."

Judge Hathorne waved to Constable Herrick who walked up to the judges' table. They whispered for a minute. Constable Herrick left and shortly returned with a disheveled man with hair nearly as wild as Goody Good's.

"I call William Good," the judge said. "Please come up to the dock."

A number of people in the room, me as well, looked surprised. I had not seen Goody Good's husband in many months. I thought he was dead or gone. I did not like that he could be compelled to testify. I shared a worried look across the room with John.

"You are Goody Good's husband?" the judge asked.

"I am."

"Is there anything about your wife that suggests that she is a witch?"

"No," Mr. Good started, but as he talked he broke down. He looked sadly at his wife and shook his head, "but may I say with tears that she is an enemy to all good."

Elizabeth repeatedly screamed which started Betty crying.

Constable Herrick removed Goody Good from the

meetinghouse.

Judge Hathorne sat in his chair. He was bored with asking the same questions and getting the same answers.

Goody Osborne struggled to stand at the dock. She was frail and needed a chair.

"Have you made a contract with the devil?" Judge Hathorne's loud, insistent voice served him well with Goody Osborne.

"No. I never saw the devil in my life."

It had been quiet for a while, but at this moment, Ann Putnam fell to the floor in convulsions. Oddly, no one, not her parents or Dr. Griggs moved to her side to ease her.

"Why do you hurt these children?" Judge Hathorne accused in an angry voice.

"I don't hurt them."

Goody Sibley came close to me and covertly touched my hand. "Why does he insist on calling them children?" she asked. "They're young women for the most part."

"Who do you employ to hurt them?" Judge Hathorne barked at Goody Osborne.

"Nobody."

"What am I to do?" I asked Goody Sibley.

"These people make no distinction between protective and healing powers as opposed to antagonistic powers. It does not matter that your intent in making the witchcake was to help the girls."

Your intent. Goody Sibley was distancing herself from her part in this.

"They believe everything is good or evil and occult practices always have harmful intent. They think occult power is always derived from devilish association."

"How are you familiar with Sarah Good?" Judge

Hathorne barked.

"I haven't spoken with her in years," Goody Osborne answered.

"They have already named you a witch," Goody Sibley said. "You are an instrument of evil or you are a victim of evil. These are your choices. You must show them that you are not at fault. They want you to show penitence, but you cannot be saved if you do not first confess. Confess or there is no hope for you and you will burn."

Judge Hawthorn yawned, hid mouth wide and open.

"I say," Goody Sibley said, "if you're going to tell them a story, make it a good one. Make them afraid of you."

20
Salem Village, March 1692

The public had grown restless after the long inquiries with Goody Good and Goody Osborne. Judge Hathorne called my name. Constable Herrick pulled me through the throng. I was made to stand at the dock, my back to the crowd. I faced the judge's table. Judge Hathorne prepared himself for his booming opening.

"So why do you hurt these children?"

"I don't hurt them. I've done nothing."

Judge Hawthorn rolled his eyes and deeply sighed.

"What does the devil tell you to make you hurt them?"

I turned my head to take in the room and found John standing at the back of the meetinghouse. He held Violet in his arms. She squirmed, tried to get down, but he held her fast. She cried, but quietly, so John gave her the twig doll.

Tell a good story, I thought. *Make them fear you.*

The Reverend Parris moved next to John and Violet. His countenance was a threat. I returned his glare. It was a face-off.

Some creatures are infected with darkness, an evil being that attacks people. He has long hair, half man, half dog with red eyes and teeth as sharp as a knife.

I took a deep breath and pointed my accusing aim across the room at the Reverend Parris.

"A devil came to me and told me that I must serve him."

Every face in the meetinghouse jerked up and began to pay attention.

The Reverend Parris scampered back to his papers. He wrote down my words.

"What? You and who else?" Judge Hathorne asked.

I took my cues from Judge Hathorne and the questions he asked, but I keep my stare on the Reverend Parris.

"A tall man that Goody Good and Goody Osborne did not see."

"That's right," Goody Good called from the back of the room. "I didn't see a tall man."

The judge ignored her. "When did you see this man?" he asked me.

I thought of the yellow warbler I had seen outside. What was his message? Why could I not get my thoughts in order?

"Birds appeared in my dreams and told me when the children were first hurt." I turned and stole a look at the audience. It was as if they had never had a dream. "And then, last night, I dreamed I was in Boston."

The room grew quiet, still, as it had not been before. I could not even hear breathing.

The judge looked stunned, incredulous. "So you did hurt the children?"

I patted the crown of my head. It throbbed and felt warm. The visions came, but not the peace. There was no peace.

I considered my answer. "I hurt children no more."

The girls were whimpering and everyone in the crowd began speaking in low tones, comparing perspectives with each other.

"Are you sorry you hurt them?"

Mr. Cheever was having difficulty hearing with the commotion in the room. "What did she say?"

"She said she hurt the children," the Reverend Parris

responded, so Mr. Cheever wrote that down.

I looked at the girls with genuine sorrow for their suffering. I wanted to help them.

"Tell us what you have seen?" Judge Hathorne asked.

"Last night there was an, uh, appearance that said if I wouldn't do as he bid he would do worse to me and mine." I couldn't say directly what devil had threatened John and Violet, but I hoped that some people might make a connection.

"What "appearance" did you see?"

John caught my gaze. He looked fearful. He shook his head, so I rethought my approach.

"What likeness came before you?" Judge Hathorne grew impatient.

"A dog. A great dog. Hairy. He stood on his hind legs like a man."

I heard an intake of breath. A few gasps. One person began to cry.

"And what did it say to you?"

"The black dog said I must serve him, but I said I was afraid. He talked of pretty things that he would give to me if I served him."

"What pretty things?"

I thought of my protection zemi burning in the fireplace. I so wanted to hold it again. It was mine and it was gone. "He didn't show me, " I answered.

I turned and looked at the anxious room. I hoped they might see. I hoped they might understand, but I was confused by the panicked looks of their faces.

"What other creatures do you see?"

"A bird."

"A bird?"

"Yes. A great winged yellow bird." I couldn't get my thoughts right. My speech had become a bit of a ramble and I could see the terror. I could see how effective that could be, so I just started making things up, saying whatever came to mind. "I saw two cats, one red and another black and as big as a dog."

"What familiar does Sarah Osborne have?"

"She only has the hairy wolf that goes upright like a man."

Elizabeth cried out and all eyes turned to her.

A few of the mothers rushed their children out of the room.

"Did you pinch Elizabeth Hubbard?"

I wondered at my actions. Could my words be spread to the protection of others? I pointed at Goody Good and Goody Osborne. "They made me pinch her."

Elizabeth fell into a fit. Pandemonium broke out as the other girls began to cry. A voice from the back of the room called out.

"Make Tituba touch her." It was Goody Putnam.

The girls became more hysterical.

The Reverend Parris said, "If the prisoner touches the children, it will put them out of their agony. I've read about it myself."

Judge Hathorne looked skeptical, but signaled for Constable Herrick to bring Elizabeth forward. I touched her gently, soothingly on the arm as I had wished to do all day. I whispered words of assurance. Elizabeth quieted.

Constable Herrick brought the other girls to be touched. I stroked away their fears. I was comforted and so were they. They settled each in turn.

"Why did you go to Thomas Putnam's house last night and hurt his child?"

I was overwhelmed, exhausted. I couldn't speak for a few seconds. I closed my eyes and fell into a brief trance. I watched the setting of the sun outside the meetinghouse windows.

"I only do what he makes me," I said.

"How did you go?"

In my head, I felt the reverend's broomstick on my back as he hit again and again. "We ride upon sticks," I said.

Judge Hathorne didn't know what to make of this. "You go through the trees or over them." There was a touch of sarcasm in his voice.

"We see nothing, but are there presently."

"Why did you not tell your master?"

"He said he would cut off my head."

"What clothes does the man wear?"

I glared at the Reverend Parris. "Black clothes." The Reverend Parris finally understood that I was accusing him, but no one else did.

The day finally ended. I heard the words that are being whispered around me as they tied me into the cart.

"Satanic pact…"

"Covenant with the devil…"

"…puts us all in jeopardy."

I didn't care. I just wanted to sleep.

Constable Herrick drove us to Ipswich to be confined for the night.

21
Ipswich, March 1692

I knew in my mind that I had made the right choice, however, my body did not understand. My fingers trembled like an old man's. I clutched them together until the knuckles turned white. My chest tightened so that I could not draw breath. I gasped and sucked in the cold night air. My anguish was so intense it scraped my nerves raw, leaving my skin feeling like an open wound. I understood that I was already dead. I had naught to do except to wait for my end.

For a second night, the three of us were kept like livestock in a pigsty. We had spent the night before chained in this place as well.

Before we arrived, the mother pig and her piglets were released to an open-air pen to wander in the churned-up mud. I could hear the happy grunts of pleasure of the babies as they wandered in between their mother's hooves. I could imagine the look of satisfaction on the mother's face as she nourished and protected her offspring.

We were kept in an airless, windowless closet meant for use as a winter smokehouse. Straw, thankfully unsullied by the pigs, covered the bloodstains on the floor where the adult hogs were bled out.

In summer, if a pig was slaughtered for food, it was immediately eaten lest it rot. If there was more meat than the family could consume, it was shared with the pastor, the doctor, the teacher, and the neighbors.

In winter, if a pig was slaughtered, it was cut into pieces

in this room, packed into a tub of coarse salt until all the water was drawn from its flesh and then the meat was hung from the roof while a small fire smoldered. The result was a salty meat that lasted through the cold months. With the coming of spring, we were the meat left in the smokehouse waiting for slaughter.

Just beyond the heavy door there were two stalls, both empty, but thick with defiled straw waiting to be mucked out. The aroma was pungent and overwhelming even through the heavy door. It left an acrid taste in my mouth that mixed well with the taste of my fear.

The two Sarahs and I sat together in aggressive silence against the tight wood planks of walls. The walls were grayed with mold, dank and offered little protection from the cold and wind that crept in from outside.

Even after eighteen years as a slave, there was still plenty I didn't understand about the people in my life. I dressed liked them and talked like them, but I was different, apart.

"What is the significance of the name Sarah?" I spoke into the darkness to fill the void in the air. I was surprised by the haunted quality of my own voice.

"It means lady or noblewoman," Goody Osborne said in a voice so quiet it was barely a whisper.

A matron entered the smokehouse and was attempting to disrobe Goody Good. Goody Good yelled and slapped. She was clearly not a noblewoman. Goody Good was considered disreputable, an outcast.

Goody Osborne was caught up in a fit of coughing. I wanted to hold her hand and rub her back to ease the spasm, but I dared not. Soon, Goody Osborne's throat relaxed of its own accord.

When the matron finished with them, Goody Good and Goody Osborne redressed themselves. I stood naked in the cold. The matron examined every inch of my body.

It was evident that the farmer's wife had recently threshed the rye in this contained area. The unknown kernels on the hay covered the floor. It's spores floated in the light of the lantern.

"What do you imagine you will find?" Goody Good asked the matron.

"Witch's teat or some other sign of the devil."

The matron's touch was very light on some of my worst wounds from my beating from the Reverend Parris. I saw the first flicker of interest in the matron's eyes, but otherwise she seemed uninvolved.

"I'll bring you a salve for these," she said. She handed my dress to me. "Is there anything else you need?"

"May we have a broom to sweep the hay from this stall?" I asked.

"You'll need that for warmth," the matron said.

"Putnam straw won't keep us warm," Goody Good nodded to me. "Comes from those with too cold a heart."

"Putnam straw?"

"I saw him haul it over here myself. To pay for a pig."

The matron was right about the cold, but I had been feeling odd all day. My feet seemed to float and my mind wandered. I think I had been seeing things that may not have been there. I may have said things that I had not intended.

As we entered the smokehouse, I was beginning to feel myself again. And now, I was back in the rye with the strange growths on it and my own feeling of strangeness was returning.

My thoughts traveled back to nights around the fire with the shaman of our village. The shaman would chop and cook the special leaves that aided him in reaching the spirit world. The shaman would go deep into himself and see things not visible to me.

"I want to know what's become of my daughter. That's

what I want," Goody Good said. Her yelling pulled me out of my reflections.

"I'll see what I can find out," the matron responded.

The matron exited as Joseph and William Porter entered. William's arms were full of heavy woolen blankets. He handed one to each of us. I walked over to receive mine. When he was done, William left.

Mr. Porter held out his hand. I looked at it in wonder. He extended it a bit further and I saw the corner of a pouch within. I shook his hand and then glanced at a small parcel in my palm.

"Goody Sibley sent this along for Goody Osborne's discomfort. All could see it at the hearing."

I hid the package in my clothes. "She does poorly," I said. "Will you ask Dr. Griggs to come?"

"As ill as his niece is, I doubt that he will."

William returned with John. From first sight, John gave me his silent comfort. I relaxed some.

"Beyond the spectral and the touch, they have no real evidence," Mr. Porter looked at my husband.

"What does that mean?" he asked.

"Spectral evidence is when the apparition appears to the girls, as they said it did in the hearing. Touch evidence is when a witch suddenly stops a fit by touching the girls."

"As I did. Those girls were starved for comfort. I gave them a little. That was all."

"Maybe if you were a bit more Christian, less contrary..." Mr. Porter said.

"I have listened to the stories that the reverend tells in church and have come to the conclusion that the Reverend Parris doesn't seem to rightly understand them."

Mr. Porter covered his grin with his hand. "I have had such thoughts myself."

"You seem to view the world as full of objects waiting to be implemented according to your will as if everything else surrounds your lives, but this is not the truth. To not be contrary, is to say that you dominate. To not be contrary, is to agree that you have ownership of the land, the trees," she paused, "and of me and my family."

Mr. Porter hung his head. He looked to John. "Be quick," he said as he walked out giving us a few moments of privacy.

I held John's hands. He looked at the other women as they settled onto the straw and fell into a restless, exhausted sleep.

"What will save me?" I asked. "That I look different from them? That I come from a home place that is strange to them? That I'm a slave in the house of a disreputable minister? That I performed white magic and made a witchcake?"

John brought my fingers to his lips.

"The Reverend Parris bid me to confess, so I tell them of my spirit dreams and convince them that I have power."

"I hear the whisperings of Goody Sibley in your words."

"She says that if I show true repentance they will forgive me, but I can't repent what I have not confessed."

John dropped his head.

I knew what he was thinking, but did not say. I, too, saw the flaw in Goody Sibley's advice.

"Are you well?" he asked. "You seemed out of sorts today."

"Yes." I said. I saw no benefit in giving John more worry.

"I hear that Mercy Lewis fell to the ground choking as she tended to Ann Putnam. They say her feet and hands twisted unnaturally and her tongue fell from her mouth. This is what you have confessed to."

"There's no taking it back now."

William nodded to John and he had to leave. He gave me one more moment of his warmth and then walked out.

The matron returned with a pitcher of milk and a loaf of rye bread. I had not eaten the bread the night before, but now I felt weak and a bit dizzy. I drank a cup of milk and nibbled on a bit of the bread. What difference did it make now?

I pushed the straw away from me and wrapped myself in the blanket. The two Sarahs huddled on my either flank so they could share my warmth through the plain, homespun dress of gray that I wore. With the exception of a slight difference in tone, my dress was the same as Goody Good's. Goody Osborne's was fancier, but less practical.

Left Sarah, Goody Good, was particularly odorous, but she favored me by keeping a little distance. She muttered foul comments under her breath. She stayed close only out of necessity, not affection.

"What's become of her?" Goody Good yelled out, but she got no answer. "Where's my daughter?" Parents loved their children. Even smelly, homeless Goody Good loved her feral offspring, a little girl of five years named Dorcas. The roundness of Goody Good's belly indicated that she had another baby on the way.

As I loved my child, I thought. What would become of my family? Where was my husband, my child? Who would care for my baby girl while I rotted away in jail? What would become of her when I died?

I didn't yell out as did Goody Good. I was convinced that I would never lay my eyes on either my husband or child again. Foremost in my mind was the question – Had I done enough to save them? Had I sacrificed myself for some purpose?

Right Sarah, Goody Osborne, was easing out of her middle years moving too fast toward old age. She was sickly and fragile. Her breath rasped deeply in and out. She shivered with chills, but her skin felt hot to the touch. Her thinking seemed to be dull, as if she was unable to discern what was happening to her.

Goody Osborne shifted her position so that she lay heavy on me, draped over me like a thick blanket. It was like when I fell asleep with John's head and arm on my chest. It was comforting until the blood settled.

A bird was caught inside me, fluttering in a panic for release. My breath wouldn't come right and the sensation of ants crawling started in my arms. The comfort past, all I wanted was to move, to shift my position, to run.

22
Salem Village, March 1692

Next morning, Judge Hathorne sat on his chair. He looked exhausted. I stood at the dock, the morning sun shining into my eyes. It was the second long day of questioning.

The meetinghouse continued to be noisy and overfull. On this day, there were more men than women and children in the pews. It seemed likely that the men insisted that their fair ladies and children stay at home. The voices had an edge. They were gruff and angry, covering fear and panic.

"What did they say when they took hold of you?" Judge Hathorne asked.

"They said to pinch Betty. I didn't want to do it. I love Betty, but they hauled me and made me pinch Betty and then Abigail."

"Did they pinch Betty?"

"No, but they all looked on."

"And what did the devil say then?"

"He said that my master had gone to prayers and he gave me a book."

My mind flashed back to the book that the harbormaster had in Barbados, and then a second harbormaster with a second book in Boston.

"Do you remember anything from this book? Was it a great book or a small book?"

"He had it in a pocket."

"Did he make you write your name in the book? Did you mark it in blood?"

The walls oozed scarlet. They dripped and then flowed. I saw this, but knew it was not real. "Yes, blood," I repeated.

Someone gasped.

"Did you see other marks in his book?"

"Yes. A great many." A wave of yellow spread like the wings of the bird. "Some were red and some were yellow."

"Did he tell you any names?"

"No names. I will not name others," I said.

The Reverend Parris leaned to Mr. Cheever and told him, "She names Goody Good and Goody Osborne, plus two more."

The Reverend Parris no longer tried to hide the fact that he was feeding falsehoods to Mr. Cheever for the official record. It was unclear to me whether Mr. Cheever was aware of this or not.

"You say there were nine of them," Judge Hathorne said.

"Yes."

"Did he tell you where the nine lived?

"Some in Boston and some in another town."

The hearings went on in this manner for five days. Questions without answers. Me rambling, out of my head, any words that crossed my mind. It ended late on the fifth night. Judge Hathorne and I sat in the nearly empty meetinghouse. With us were Mr. Cheever, the Reverend Parris, and Constable Herrick with two of his men.

Judge Herrick stood and pointed at Mr. Cheever. "Take this down," he ordered. He composed his thoughts for a moment and then began, "Tituba, an Indian woman, servant to Samuel Parris of Salem Village wickedly and feloniously entered into a covenant with the devil and made a mark in the devil's book. She, the said Tituba, became a detestable witch against

156

the crown and the laws of the state."

He looked aggravated as he waved his hand in the air. He pointed to Constable Herrick. "Take her."

23

Ipswich, March 1692

Constable Herrick shuffled me into the jail cell in the pigsty. The cell was freezing and Goody Osborne stumbled on the smelly straw and shivered with a fever.

"May we have an extra blanket for her? She's not well."

Constable Herrick watched as I settled Goody Osborne. He picked up heavy shackles and held them in his left hand.

Goody Osborne was shaking and shivering, likely not just with the cold. I touched my hand to her forehead. She was on fire. She struggled to gain breath, sucking in short gasps, and then turned and vomited on the straw.

I saw Goody Good crinkle her nose. We both understood that this was a smell we would have all night. To her credit, Goody Good did not comment. She moved some unsullied straw over the sick.

"What happens now?" demanded Goody Good. "What happens to me?" Goody Good sat down at my side.

"The written record of your testimony and the statements of the witnesses will be sent to the grand jury to decide if this case comes to trial or not."

This was disturbing news as I felt certain the written record was at best misleading and at worst quite untruthful.

Constable Herrick pulled on Goody Good's arms to move them closer together. He shackled first one wrist and then the other.

"And what do I do? Wait in chains until I'm forgotten?"

It seemed preposterous to Goody Good that she should be forced into a life against her will, forced to go where she did not wish, act in a manner she did not wish, but that was the life I'd had for the past eighteen years.

Constable Herrick locked the chains on me. "Those girls say that you fly to them at night."

I forced myself not to shy away.

I closed my eyes and said good-bye to all that is good. I said good-bye in my heart to John and Violet.

"Tomorrow," he said. "I'll move you three to Salem Town." He looked at me. "They have a real jail there."

Constable Herrick took the lantern as he walked out the door. I sat there in the frigid dark.

Goody Osborne coughed.

24
Salem Town, March 1692

Five days after our arrest, we were moved to the jail in Salem Town to await trial. We were loaded onto the cart, our hands and feet bound, and jostled the four miles down the road from the farming village to the main town. The road was little more than a cleared dirt path with trees and boulders removed.

We made a parade as we passed curious, scared and unhappy populaces along the road. I nodded my head and smiled to let them know me, remember me. I think that scared them more. So, I concentrated instead on my backside and wrists, both of which hurt with each bump and tussle with the road. The bird in my chest pounded against my ribs and my muscles jumped of their own accord.

Once near Salem Town, the buildings increased in number and relation to the road. The road became more wide and flat. We passed a tree-lined common, the county courthouse and a school where children entered a wooden doorway. There were shops, mills and houses. It felt unreal to see common life still going on.

My teeth rattled in my head as the cart headed down the cobbled streets toward the town's center. Each jolt brought fresh tears to my eyes.

The jail itself was a house in the middle of the city. A part of the yard was surrounded with a tall split-rail fence where two guards stood. I imagined myself confined to that limited rectangle of movement. I wanted to scream.

Centered in the fenced yard was a fire pit used to make

the prisoners' food. One of the guards hung a large cauldron over a small flame. The foul smell was overwhelming.

The jail's outer walls were made of wood planks like any house. It had high windows with no iron bars. With some effort, it might be possible to escape. Puritans weren't supposed to run from their sins, and so they rarely did.

Inside, the cells were partitioned off rooms with wood plank walls. Each had its own spiked door. The hallway was dark as constant night. I was walked by a guard down a corridor bordered on one side by several small rooms. The guard kept his distance from me and never made direct eye contact.

The guard taunted me. "Those be the cells for inmates who are dangerous or demented."

The opposite wall had a few more cells.

The guard continued. "Those be for prisoners who pay for a little more luxury." He sneered as his foot came down on a cockroach. "Means we stomp the kackerlacka for you."

The three of us were shoved into a common area. The large compartment had the potent smells of humanity left unchecked for too long a period. It smelled of body odor, sour food and urine. The walls did little to shelter us from the cold. There was straw on the floor just like the pigsty in Ipswich, however I saw no obvious evidence of fungus. One tiny window stood about five feet from the floor on the outside wall. In the corner, there was a barrel with water and a tin cup. Nearby was an empty bucket. I had no money to buy straw or a blanket to keep me warm at night. I moved toward the window where I knew its light would warm me for at least a portion of the day.

A tall man with no hair on his head, but bushy eyebrows, showed Goody Osborne into her new home. He introduced himself to her as Mr. Lovell. He had kind eyes the same color blue as the Caribbean Sea.

Goody Good yelled wildly in defiance. She shook the bars of the door and kicked at the walls.

"Calm yourself or I'll put the shackles on," the other guard said. This was the first I noticed iron shackles attached to a few feet of chain, a pair located every couple feet along all the walls.

"That's Mr. Ingesson," Mr. Lovell said. "Don't cross him. He's known for his foul temper."

Goody Osborne lay on the straw. I brought her a little water from the barrel and sat quietly near her. Soon, she fell asleep while I held her hand.

In the morning, the sun shone against my eyelids. It made a red and orange pattern, the color of fire and rage. I could hear a guard calling, even before I was fully awake. I opened my heavy, bleary eyes and looked at the guard. He was not the guard of the kind eyes. It was Mr. Ingesson, the guard of all sharp angles. His eyes, the color of bark, were intense.

"Tituba," he called. "Bring the bucket."

During the night, the bucket had been filled with a stinking, steamy mass.

"Still a slave," I thought. I purposefully ignored him and closed my eyes.

He grabbed my arm and pulled me to standing.

Confinement, incarceration, and imprisonment—these words keep rushing through my mind. I can't live in a cage, I thought. I can't live in a cage!

In a couple of weeks, Goody Martha Corey joined our number. Goody Corey had made the mistake of questioning the testimony of the afflicted girls. In particular, she challenged Ann's mother, also named Ann—Goody Ann Putnam.

We were surprised to see Goody Corey when she was dragged in. She was a senior woman in her seventies, a respected member of the church and her husband was a large landowner, but that did her no good against accusations from Ann, Abigail, Mercy, and Elizabeth.

"I told them I could not be the specter she named." Goody Corey pointed an accusing finger at me. "My own clothing was not the same as *she* described, so Mr. Cheever set up a clothing test for young Ann. He examined my clothing and then went to young Ann to have her describe it."

"What happened?" Goody Good asked.

Clearly, Mr. Lovell was interested in the answer to that question as well as he had hung back and puttered around the water barrel.

"When Mr. Cheever confronted Ann, she said that I had blinded her." Goody Corey received the expression of outrage that she expected. She huffed. She spotted Mr. Lovell at the water barrel. "I want some water," she demanded.

Mr. Lovell huffed in return and left the cell.

Goody Corey was a convener at the Salem church. She had married well. She and Mr. Corey owned property. Goody Corey thought she had station. She was an outspoken woman, used to getting her own way. But I had listened to words spoken in whispers about her. Goody Corey's son was illegitimate and a mulatto. To me, Goody Corey seemed naïve about her situation and clearly wrongheaded in her brash and entitled approach to the guards. That was her problem. I kept my mouth shut about it.

Goody Good screamed night and day for her daughter, Dorcas. Goody Good and Dorcas had been living hard on their own before our arrest. Since there was nothing to do with Dorcas now, they brought her to the jail.

Dorcas was five years old. At best, Dorcas whined and flitted around the cell. At worst, she sobbed until I didn't know if I wanted to tear my heart from my breast or hers from her. Dorcas was confused and terrified, so I tried to be mindful of that.

Dorcas was brought in with Goody Rebecca Nurse, an elderly gentlewoman. Goody Nurse had spoken in defense of Goody Elizabeth How. With accusations proliferating, Goody Nurse must have known such words might be dangerous. She seemed a woman of tremendous courage.

Goody Nurse was quite old and could hear nearly nothing. She huddled in a corner in fear and confusion. The old, the sick and the unwanted -- they were making a purge.

"Tituba. Tell me a story," Dorcas commanded in a tone she had learned from her mother. I had told her, had told all the children, many stories, but I was of no mind to entertain at this moment.

Goody Good favored me with her own stern look.

Dorcas had slept little and, when she did, she ground her teeth together until her jaw hurt. In her waking hours, she was lashed out in every direction.

"It might soothe her," Goody Osborne said.

I held out my arms and Dorcas came to me. I smoothed her tangled hair as I began.

"Our village was on a river that reached out in many directions like a spider's web. The river was called Orinoco. During part of the day, the waters of the river were high covering the trees and shrubs that lined the bank. When the waters returned to the ocean, the air smelled of salt. Once I tasted the dirt and it was salty too."

Dorcas snickered. "You ate dirt."

"I was small then, like you. I lived on the river with my tribe, many of whom were my kin. I had my mother, my father and two sisters."

I continued. "When the brackish water returned to the

ocean, my mother and I ran barefoot through the mangrove to the water's edge to collect oysters." And no one said it was unseemly or ungodly to remove our shoes and caps, I thought.

"Oysters. What are they?" Dorcas asked.

"There's a shell and inside meat you can eat." I answered in a distracted way as I was thinking about my mother. "My mother was beautiful. She had shiny hair, black as a panther. It hung down her back. I loved to run my fingers through its length to pull out the tangles." I ran my fingers through Dorcas's hair in the same manner.

"So she looked like you then?" Goody Osborne noted.

"Compared to you, yes, she did. She was small with skin the color of burnt sugar. Her black eyes were shaped like almonds."

"Stop. You're making me hungry."

But I wasn't listening. "My mother wore a colored cloth like a skirt that she tied at her waist with a rope. She often carried a basket on her back that she had woven herself. The basket I liked best was decorated with pictures of monkeys at the top and frogs at the bottom."

Dorcas chittered at the mention of monkeys. I had told her of them in the past and taught her to make the noises of jungle animals. Dorcas danced around the cell curling her fingers into her armpits. The others laughed, but I scarcely noticed. Soon she wore herself out and returned to my side.

"My mother wore a necklace made of seeds and feathers around her neck." I touched an empty spot at the base of my neck. My throat grew tight as I held back tears.

Goody Osborne sat taller and blinked a few times. "She's resting now," she said of Dorcas, who was nestled in my arms in a manner that hid her face from me.

Dorcas had cried through the previous night. I was glad she slept. I was glad to hold her in my arms. I lay my head back against the wall and closed my eyes. I held Dorcas as I also held my mother's memory.

Mr. Lovell brought in a tasteless gruel. He handed us each a plate. I set mine aside knowing that I would be hungry enough at a later time to eat it.

Mr. Lovell retrieved a bucket from outside the cell and filled the water barrel. He took the other barrel, the private barrel, outside the cell to empty it.

Outside the jail's window, Mr. Ingesson stirred gruel in a large, heavy iron pot. Mr. Ingesson was a tall, absurdly thin man with a long hooked nose. He had a sour disposition and a sharp tongue. He reminded me of the seaman who also brought us a tasteless gruel and emptied piss pots.

"Why must I be the one to do this?" Mr. Ingesson complained.

As was my habit, I stood inside the window watching the citizens of Salem Town going about their business. We were near the city center, close to houses, stores and the Essex County courthouse.

Mr. Ingesson spotted me at the window. He came inside and pulled me out. "You," he said. "Make your own dinner."

I stirred the cereal he had started and took a tentative sniff. "Sir," for that is all he wished to be called. "May we please have a little salt?"

"You be making some sort of witches potion? Ja?"

"With salt? I just want to make it taste a bit better."

Mr. Ingesson gave me a scornful look, but retired to the kitchen and returned with salt and two plants he'd pulled up by the roots from the kitchen garden.

I used a few top leaves from the herbs and planted the remainder of the basil and oregano in a rusted-out cast iron pot I filled with loose dirt.

Mr. Lovell and Mr. Ingesson ate brown meat and a little johnnycake. Mr. Ingesson seemed to like Mr. Lovell about as well as he liked me. But, to me, Mr. Lovell had the aspect of a kind man, softly spoken, with an awareness of me few others had.

Mr. Ingesson sniffed the air. "Why does their food smell better than mine?"

I pinched a little salt between my fingertips and held it over his meat. I waited for him to give his concurrence before I let the grains drift from my fingertips onto his food.

He took a bite. Nodded. "You've earned yourself a new job."

That was fine by me. Outside, in the fresh air, I was happy with that.

Later, Mr. Lovell and I cleaned up.

"Tell me about your homeland," I asked him.

"My homeland? I'm a traveler. I have no home."

I truly wanted to know him. "Where were you born? Where do your parents live?"

"My parents were from the lowlands of Scotland until they fled to England to avoid being hanged. We were there until the king needed exports for the second settlement of Nova Scotia—new Scotland.

"I've heard of Nova Scotia. North of here across an invisible line."

This brought a smile to Mr. Lovell's face. "We had to expel the French from Port Royal and we did, but when Charles I came to power, he gave Nova Scotia back to the French. And so soon enough, I ended up here."

I glanced toward Mr. Ingesson as he guarded the door to the jail. "And him?"

"Ingesson comes from Sweden. He came to Dutch-ruled New Netherland, but the English attacked and took over the Dutch and Swedish colonies."

"Scotland. Sweden." I was confused and it showed on my face. "So many tribes."

"Countries, not tribes. How to explain? The world is a considerable size, larger than you can imagine. Across the sea, invisible lines divide the world as you say. We thought we knew how big the world was, but then we found more lands toward the sunrise and then more lands beyond that. And in the east they had many things that we wanted."

"Like horses and guns?"

"Something like that. It's really far to travel overland to the east, so an English man teamed up with the Spanish queen and sailed west to see if he could find a shorter route. His ships ran into a new land instead. Your land. This land is also much bigger than you may know and so they started dividing it up with invisible lines. Spain, Portugal, France, many countries—all took ownership of parts of your land."

I listened, but would leave understanding to later.

"For them, land means independence," Mr. Lovell said. "Without it, they could become servants or slaves. Like us.

"You're no slave."

"Anyone without property is considered the same as a slave."

25

Salem Town, April 1692

Memories flooded my day and dreams invaded my night. John came out of the turquoise water and smiled at me. Violet played with the twig doll in its yellow dress and blue shawl. Betty read her Bible by the red evening fire. Yessi waded in the blue river and sang the shaman's chants in a high, clear voice. Mrs. Duville created her hats with purple feathers and Mrs. Pearsehouse arranged flowers of every color in a vase in her morning room. My mother reached toward me before she disappeared into a white nothing.

But, they only came in sleep. John did not visit. He did not bring Violet. I wanted to assume that he was not allowed to see me. I knew this was likely so, but still I felt hurt.

Goody Parris also did not come and bring my family or hers. I heard much of Betty at the start, but no more. I wanted to believe she had not died, that she felt better and had returned to being a little girl. I missed her almost as much as I missed Violet.

Goody Sibley did not come to visit me with a basket of herbs or a soothing tonic.

The Porters no longer brought me an extra blanket.

I was forgotten.

Mr. Lovell did appear. He unlocked the spiked door. He wanted me to cook the evening meal. He had a sly smile on his face.

"Happy Easter," he said.

"What's that?" I asked without much interest.

As we stepped into the yard, I was taken with beautiful spring sunshine and clear, blue sky. Two small trees near the splitrail fence budded. Green grass and flowers poked through damp ground in the yard.

"You remember Jesus from the reverend's teachings?"

"I do."

"Easter is a day we celebrate his life. The Puritans set aside Sunday for worship, but they think every day is blessed. They don't celebrate any holy days. But I'm Catholic, so I do."

Mr. Lovell held up a fine, big turkey. Its feathers were already plucked. "Brought you something special to cook for the prisoners. Can you prepare it?"

I nodded.

"Is a turkey a difficult bird to hunt?" I asked.

"Wouldn't know. I purloined it at the market." Mr. Lovell studied me. "There you go again looking at me like I'm the strange one."

"If you lived more with nature, not constantly fighting against it, maybe you wouldn't need to be a jailor."

"I won't be a jailor forever."

I thought about Betty as I prepared the first meat the prisoners had seen in two months. Betty loved turkey meat roasted slowly over a fire and then covered in coarse salt distilled from the sea.

"Have you heard anything of Betty Parris?" I asked Mr. Lovell.

"I don't remember from whom, but I heard the Reverend Parris sent her away to live elsewhere."

"That's good," I said. I nodded my head and breathed a slight sigh of relief for her.

Betty, Abigail, and Elizabeth had been truly sick. I had held their sweating bodies as they convulsed in unnatural ways and vomited. I know that, at the least, Elizabeth saw things that were not there.

When the two Sarahs and I were in the pigsty in Ipswich during the hearings, I felt off. I think we all did. Not as sick as the girls, not yet, but not like ourselves. This feeling went away in a few days after we were moved to Salem Town.

These girls spent hours of every day in the shed with the rye. They fed the horse, cleaned and mucked her stall. They curried her; especially Betty took her time grooming Star's coat. They brought the horse treats to eat. And they played in the rye. Anytime the girls wished to escape the notice of their parents or have a quiet moment alone, they went to the shed.

In the Putnam house, I had heard many things about Ann that made me believe she might be genuinely ill. Maybe Mercy as well, but she was conniving enough to lie to meet whatever aim she pleased.

Mercy had teamed up, probably with ill intent, with another servant from the household of a farmer and tavern keeper and his wife, John and Elizabeth Proctor. The servant was named Mary Warren, who seemed even more angry and sly than Mercy.

This proved to be true when soon enough Goody Elizabeth Proctor was arrested and brought into the jail. Goody Proctor was a slight woman with a pensive demeanor.

"My husband had not liked Mary's involvement with the afflicted girls," Goody Proctor said. He's quick to temper," she confided in a quiet tone, as if she didn't say it loudly it would be as if she hadn't spoken against her husband at all.

I took that to mean that he may have taken the Reverend Parris's method to resolve his concerns and tried to strike the fits out of Mary. In a minute, she confirmed this.

"He used his riding crop to make her behave."

I supposed she had never said this out loud before.

Maybe she felt well away from him.

"He went out of town and she was fine in his absence, but by his return Mary had accused me of sending a specter to torment her. I don't know what I ever did to offend her."

I shared her pain until she turned on me.

"Your husband named me as a witch," she said.

"He wouldn't do that," I responded. "John's a quiet man. John wouldn't volunteer comment much less accusation. He just would not."

Unless he was protecting Violet. I thought about the threats the Reverend Parris made to me. John would say or do anything to protect his baby girl.

I wanted to believe he would take Violet away if she was in danger.

Unless he could not. I pictured him in my mind in shackles and chains, whipped and beaten down. Humiliated.

Less than a week later, Mr. John Proctor was arrested and brought into the jail. He was a lone man among nearly a dozen women. He had been arrested for witchcraft in much the same manner as everyone else, but his maleness made him unique.

To protect himself, he had thirty-one people sign a petition saying that they had never seen him perform witchcraft. When that didn't work, he appealed to a group of Boston clergy, but nothing helped him.

Mr. Proctor kept to himself, not saying much about what brought about his circumstances, except to note that he was protecting his family from his serving girl Mary Warren, who had fits and blamed them on the witchcraft of his wife and then himself.

Goody Proctor didn't look as if she felt protected. She immediately took her place beside her husband, but she retreated into herself, rarely speaking again. She lost all personality.

It was an awkward and unhappy reunion when Mr. Giles Corey was brought to jail. Mr. Corey was older than his wife, he being at least eighty years of age. He had a habit of clearing phlegm from his throat and spitting which I found particularly annoying. When he spoke, his words came out as if they stuck inside. They traveled a coarse and graveled path up his throat.

Neither Mr. nor Goody Corey was given to restraint. They took corners on opposite sides of the cell and yelled unkind words across the space at each other.

"I defended you," Mr. Corey yelled to her in his craggy voice.

"You testified against me. Right from the start, that judge assumed that I was guilty. He made that clear with every question," Goody Corey shouted. "I told him I was a good woman, but he didn't care."

I knew exactly what she meant. Judge Hathorne was the same with me, with us all.

"I heard what happened at the Putnam house." Mr. Corey said. "I heard that, when you visited, both Ann and Mercy fell into fits and you were asked to leave. What was I to think? It sounded like witchcraft to me."

"That judge wanted to know how I knew about the clothes test. I told them I figured it out. They didn't think me clever enough."

I had had trouble describing the clothes of the specter that haunted me. It was an issue in my hearing as well. You did not have to be too clever to guess that they had incorporated the clothes test into the next hearing.

"They didn't believe me, so I told them you told me.

That you had overheard in the village. They named me a witch. Do you know why? Because you didn't support my story, you spoke out against me."

"The ox laid down and then the cat died." Mr. Corey offered by way of explanation. "I thought…." He paused to gather his thoughts. "I didn't know it was a trick."

"So why are you here?" Goody Corey asked. "If you thought me a witch, why were you arrested?"

"I changed my story."

Eventually Goody Corey inched toward Mr. Corey. They whispered together in the corner until it was clear that Goody Corey had forgiven her husband.

Goody Nurse buried her head and her hands and moaned as first her sister, Sarah Cloyce, and then her other sister, Mary Easty, were brought into the jail.

"What are you doing here?" she moaned as Mr. Ingesson brought in Goody Easty. "You don't even live in Salem Village."

Goody Easty was at least a decade younger than her sister, maybe more. She was calm when she first saw their accommodations, but was also clearly unhappy about it.

Mr. Corey provided a response to Goody Nurse, "Your sisters walked out on a sermon by the Reverend Parris in protest for your arrest. I guess the good reverend didn't much care for that."

Goody Nurse's two sisters lived in Topsfield, a small community about five miles from Salem Village. Citizens of Topsfield had no interest in the Reverend Parris spreading his witchcraft fever to their community. All three sisters were well liked and their friends came to visit them in jail. They brought food and blankets that the sisters were happy to share.

Goody Easty's friends soon secured her release. She

came around to each person in the jail to say good-bye. She checked in with me.

"How are you faring?" she asked, but didn't wait for a reply. "May I take a message to someone for you? May I bring something to you?" she asked.

"Tell my family I love them," I said. I confessed to save John and Violet. Not me. "No. It's likely best that they forget about me."

Goody Easty patted my hand. "I'll bring you a little something. Maybe my special buns and jams."

"Yes. Thank you. That would be nice."

But, two days later, after the next round of assault by the accusers, Goody Easty was back in the jail.

"Mercy stepped up her campaign against me," Goody Easty explained, "and finally the others capitulated."

Goody Easty did not bring any jam.

Abigail Hobbs, also from Topsfield, soon joined our number. Abigail was fourteen years old and had been living with her parents. She was mild, but seemed to have a toughness of spirit. This is the story that Abigail told us.

"I was examined and immediately confessed."

Abby was the first to confess to witchcraft since me. I had to wonder why she did this. I was protecting my family, but what would she have to gain?

"Abigail Williams, Ann Putnam, Mercy Lewis, and Mary Warren were in the court as my accusers, but stayed silent during the proceedings."

"I would think that was unusual for them," I said.

"They even spoke words of compassion to the justices for me. For you see, I had struck a deal with them. They were my friends. They would speak for me and I would be set free."

"By the end of the hearings, only Mercy remained as my

accuser. She broke her word to me."

"What happened? I asked. The outcome seemed clear as Abigail was in the jail with the rest of us.

"My bargain may have softened my fate, but it didn't change it. There were forces beyond my friends, and not supernatural ones either. It seems that once you are accused, you will be indicted, whatever transpires in the interim."

This seemed a travesty and the numbers of cellmates grew as we listened to Abby tell her story.

Abby continued. "Shortly, they brought my stepmother to the hearings."

"Deliverance. Oh no," someone said.

"Yes. The justices kept her name secret from Mercy and then asked her to name the witch, but she could not. Mercy had said that she had seen a specter, but Mercy could not name it as my stepmother. The justices continued to speak of my stepmother's involvement with witchcraft. The justices did not care that Mercy had not passed their little test. So, Mama charged Mercy as a witch. You know what the justices did?"

Abby's rapt audience waited. No one had tried turning the accusations around, naming the accusers as the witches.

"Nothing," Abby said. "They ignored her. Later, my father told me it would confuse their cases with us and maybe start a trend they could not control in future. The justices made a choice and not for our benefit."

This was no longer about the love and fear that parents had for their sick children. I thought about whom I perceived to be truly ill and whom I did not. The one thing we all shared—the Parris family, the Griggs family, and the Putnam's—was use of the field with the rye tainted with the yellow mucus. The sickness came from that tainted harvest.

Goody Sibley and I had dismissed it as nothing. I had not seen it as a blessing from the spirits to see within our soul like the plants the shaman's used. Nor had I seen it as an evil to make the weak and vulnerable act in fear.

The Reverend George Burroughs also came in at the last of the month. The Reverend Burroughs was a formidable man, tall, and imposing. He had great muscles that stretched at his clothing.

He came at me, just as Goody Proctor had. "You named a dark man. You started Parris on a witch hunt and soon enough he rested his focus on me."

"I meant him," I explained. "Why doesn't anybody understand that? He's the dark man."

The Reverend Burroughs accused and I backed up toward the wall. "You have cost me everything. Witch or no, you are evil."

Mr. Lovell stepped between us even though I had not seen him enter the jail cell. From the expression on the Reverend Burroughs face, he had not either.

Mr. Lovell's eyes turned into a stormy fury. He removed a baton from his waist that I had never once seen him use. He stretched his arm out toward this bulk of a man and the Reverend Burroughs took a step back.

From out in the hall, I heard a snicker that could only be Mr. Ingesson. That defused the situation. The Reverend Burroughs stomped away to an opposite wall, but when the guards had left, his demeanor made it clear that this was not over.

By the time the Reverend Burroughs came into our cell, there were seven men accused, arrested, and jailed. I wondered if they all were a response to my words. And I wasn't the only one.

My interactions with my cellmates had gotten quite cold and distant. Unlike them, I did not even have the company of the other prisoners. I could not share my misery. The more people who entered the cell, the more I kept still, silent and to myself.

Husbands and wives, sisters, mothers and daughters. These people knew each other. They lived together in a small community that had been tight, close-knit. My village had been that way, a group of related families. My parents. My sisters. My aunts and uncles. We all loved each other. I could not imagine my family ever acting so with each other.

One day, a beautiful Indian woman in ill-fitting English clothes walked up to my window. She wore a hooded cape even though the weather had taken a sharp turn to warmer. She stood silently, waiting outside, until I appeared at the sill.

Her smile was soft, warm, and genuine. She lifted a flexible basket and slipped it through the window to me. The basket had a complex jaguar design. My own design. My own basket. The basket was full of fresh huckleberries.

The jaguar is the spirit of bravery and fearlessness, the shaman told me.

Huckleberries strengthen the blood, I heard Goody Sibley speaking in my mind.

The Indian woman held my hand for a moment and I knew that this woman was the wife of Ahanu. She was the wife of John's friend.

She did not speak, but I understood the message. John was fine. John had not forgotten me. John loved me. He wanted me to be brave and have strength like my spirit guide, the jaguar.

Tears moistened my eyelashes as I watched the ethereal spirit of this lovely woman walk away.

I had not offered to share the berries she had brought to me, but many hands dug into the basket. Soon it was empty.

I did not care.

I was not forgotten.

26
Salem Town, May 1692

The jail was as full as it could get, almost all women save for seven men. There were more prisoners than I could count. It was close. The air was stale and full of the smells of too many people I never wished to know. Most of the inmates put some distance between themselves and me, but some could not be ignored.

The sound of Bridget Bishop's crying filled the air. Goody Bishop's behavior was erratic and irritating. One minute, she was restless and irritable. She talked non-stop and never seemed to require sleep. The next minute, she was sad, crying and sleeping all the time.

I concentrated on the sounds I could hear outside my window. I could hear the wind lazily rustling the tops of tall trees and the scraping of tiny toenails as a chipmunk or squirrel circled the bark. I could make out three songs of birds, two called to each other in a whistling twitter while the third was a kind of hooting sound. I heard a dog bark in the distance, territorial but not angry.

Unlike the whispering, the constant whispering. The voices in low tones were angry. I opened my eyes.

The couple John and Elizabeth Procter teamed with the couple Martha and Giles Corey. This was an odd pairing as there had been some bad blood between Mr. Proctor and Mr. Corey in the past. Mr. Proctor had testified against Mr. Corey when he was accused of beating a man.

It seemed that they had resolved their differences in jail.

I guess they found common ground, and now, the four of them spent every day centered on glaring in my direction and making comments at my expense.

I heard Goody Proctor whisper John's name to Goody Corey. They wanted me to be incensed at John's flawed character and wrong actions, but I didn't know or care if their claims were true.

I sat under my window near Goody Easty. I heard the wind pick up. The sky turned gray and, in a minute, the first sounds of rain started. At first it was a light patter, but soon turned into a pouring deluge. I heard the sounds of rushing water pouring like a river down the street outside. I heard foul words from the driver of a cart. I could imagine the cart stuck in mud and the driver rocking it to pull it out.

Goody Easty had a book with pictures in it. I looked over her shoulder to better see. There was a drawing of a woman of means. She was seated in a fine room next to a table set for tea. Goody Easty's head was lowered as the woman in the drawing's head was lowered to read a book of her own. Goody Easty casually moved the volume so that I could better view it.

"Who is she?"

"An English lady."

Goody Easty turned the page and a new drawing appeared. This picture was bordered on the edges by the leaves of trees. The leaves opened into a view of a large house.

"An English country manor," Goody Easty said.

"I once saw a street full of houses so huge in Boston."

"It's small by some standards." She turned to another page and showed me a much larger stone structure. "It's called a castle."

"And the whole tribe lives inside?"

"One family. In this case," she ran her finger across some words, words I was not allowed to learn to read, "it says there is a father, mother with two children and her mother—the grandmother. There are five people in all. Of course, there would be servants. It doesn't say how many." She took a long pause as she examined the drawing with yearning and sorrow. "You know that many of the people who live here are from a faraway place."

"Mr. Lovell has told me some," I said.

"I expect that Mr. Lovell's experience of faraway places was very different from my own."

I remembered Mr. Lovell's story of escape. "Why did you come?" I asked Goody Easty.

"We believed that the leaders of our church were bad people. We sought to purify our religion, move our dreams into action, but unlike some other Puritans we did not separate from the rule of England."

"So this is why we wait for an English governor to decide our fate."

"You're very bright. I hadn't expected that. I wish I had known you a bit before, but that would never have happened as we are also very different, and…."

"I have my own ways."

"Yes, your own ways. Do you believe in God?"

"I believe in something good."

"We believe that our covenant is with God, that our faith must be active and punishment for sins is a proper response for moral disobedience.

"Who decides what is sin?"

"God." Goody Easty looked away, not letting me see her eyes. "As interpreted by men. God chooses who will receive grace and who will not, but men decide what is right and wrong behavior in his name."

This I knew and understood.

Goody Osborne lay on the ground. Her skin was yellow and she had trouble breathing. We stayed apart from others. Surprisingly, Goody Good, now huge with child, stayed closest to us, Dorcas nestled in her arms. Goody Osborne tossed in a fever dream.

"Now, now." Goody Good said as she patted her arm. She made a little cooing sound not unlike the third bird.

Edward Bishop and his wife, Sarah, stood at the spiked bars of the hallway door talking to an elderly man also called Edward Bishop. The elder Mr. Bishop dripped water from the brim of his hat and the shoulders of his coat were damp. So far as I could tell, the couple was no relation to Bridget Bishop.

"Sheriff Corwin and his deputies took the cows," elderly Edward Bishop said. "They took the chickens and the feed and tools. They confiscated everything. Said it was for the crown, but he kept everything."

"No." Younger Edward Bishop looked shocked, his anger sharpened by his inability to do anything about Sheriff Corwin or the confiscation.

"It's out of hand—the accusations, arrests, examinations, and imprisonments. The sheriff says you owe five pounds for each of you and ten shillings per week for boarding at the jail. How are you supposed to pay when Sheriff Corwin has taken all your wealth for himself? How will you pay?" he repeated.

I took in this bad news. Edward and Sarah Bishop may find a way to pay the fees, but I never would. I understood more clearly than ever that I would never leave this jail. This was home for the rest of my life.

"What news is there?" Goody Good asked Mary Black, one of the latest to be jailed.

Mary was the only other person of color in the jail. She was an African slave. Mary was cautious and so had stayed aloof since she had arrived. Mary did not answer.

Outside, the rain stopped as quickly as it started. I heard a hawk's predatory cry in the distance. The dog's bark became more insistent. The wind blew through the trees, but the other birds had gone silent.

"The plague spreads," said Mr. Edwards Sr. "Now it's not just the children, but many people, children and adults alike, who complain of the strange attacks. They point this way and that, looking for answers."

I closed my eyes for a moment and saw the dog stand on hind legs and turn into a man. His red eyes glared in my direction out of a supernatural blackness.

I opened my eyes and it was daytime again. The sky had brightened.

"Does no one speak for us?" Goody Good asked.

"I hear that the Porters spoke out against the trials until someone named one of their kin as a witch. They're not so quick to protest now."

"What of my husband?" Goody Good asked Mary. A few heads turned as if surprised that she would care what had become of her husband who testified against her, but, so long locked up with us, she had revealed her goodness to me. She likely loved her husband.

"I've not heard." Mary's black eyes rested on me. "Her husband is the slave that helped to make the witchcake?"

Goody Good nodded and my heart began to race. Blood rushed to my head.

"Do they suspect him?" I asked. "Is he in danger?" I glanced at the Proctors, recognizing that danger is everywhere.

"No. He's sick. He was shaking out some empty bags of rye when he coughed, gasped, and staggered across the barroom floor at Ingersoll's or so it's told. He was unable to walk a straight line. Nate Ingersoll was suspicious, but the other men in the tavern had a laugh at his expense. Then, he fell to the floor in a fit. Four men were required to hold him down as he seized."

I was horrified. "Who will care for him?"

I remembered the girls' shaking fits, contortions of their bodies, fever and applied these symptoms to my strong husband. The air seemed to leave the room. There was none to be had.

Goody Good patted my hand and said, "now, now."

"I don't think it will matter much longer," Mary said. "It's said that trials will soon begin."

Goody Osborne shivered and gasped.

The prisoners were divided into two camps so far as Goody Osborne was concerned. Those on their knees in a circle around me who wanted to help, but didn't know what to do. And those who wanted to stay as far away from Goody Osborne as possible.

I retrieved my blanket and lay it gently on Goody Osborne. Goody Good, and Mary Black followed suit. I was back on my knees. Goody Osborne whispered. I leaned down to hear her, but I couldn't understand the words.

Silently, I attempted to bring myself to a trance-like state, to call on the good spirits to help.

Goody Clinton watched from across the room and followed what she thought was my example and began to pray.

Mary Black, who feared death, but was too brave to be in the fear-death corner said, "Do you suppose she has what's going around outside?"

Goody Good said, "She's dying from being sick, cold, and hungry. That's all."

Mary Black took a step closer to look.

Goody Osborne shuddered, let out a final breath and died. She lay still and cold as the light shifted in the cell. Gloom surrounded her.

I checked for breath a second time, and then, pulled myself up the wall and took a couple steps away. I was shaking, afraid my knees would give way. I took another shuffling step back. If Goody Osborne had died in jail, any of us could.

Mary Black called the guards who stood outside the cell for a minute discussing. Mr. Ingesson pointed at Mary and me meaning for the two of us to pick up Goody Osborne.

Goody Clinton prayed, "Yeah though I walk through the valley of the shadow death…."

Mary pulled the blankets off of Goody Osborne and, in a dizzy fog, she and I carried Goody Osborne outside. We set her without ceremony on a patch of grass. I stood clutching my hands and looking at her. Goody Osborne was the first to know what it was to never again leave this cell.

27
Salem Town, June 1692

The sun broke hot and wasted no time climbing to its zenith. Everything was still and quiet, as if it was too cloyingly hot for people to continue persecuting their neighbors. We took a pause, both inside the jail and out.

The Reverend Burroughs had long since removed his jacket and rolled up his sleeves. As he frequently did in the morning, he read to us from his Bible. He would read some words and then explain to us what he believed the words meant.

When he first arrived, his words were all about the nature of evil and how witches should not be allowed to live. The Reverend Burroughs seemed to struggle with whether or not I was the one true witch. At the start, he spent much of his time listening to Mr. Proctor, but eventually he seemed to set his ill will aside.

Today his words came from Jeremiah. "...if you do not oppress the alien, the orphan, and the widow, or shed innocent blood in this place, then you will be with the Lord...."

The Reverend Burroughs read about a people that were sent into exile. He took great pains to explain that our situation was similar to them. While most of us had travelled little more than four miles, we were still exiled by our people. I liked the Reverend Burroughs's explanations better than the Reverend Parris's.

The jail had filled beyond capacity and so some of the arrested were moved to be confined elsewhere. We heard from

Mr. Lovell that more than a hundred people were stored in surrounding jails and buildings.

Like the pigsty, I thought.

In the month past, the new governor had come from England. Mr. Lovell had heard rumors that something might happen, but then he told us that the new governor preferred slaughtering Indians in the Indian Wars to dealing with the witchcraft crisis. I worried about Ahanu and his wife, but had heard nothing to indicate that there was fighting in the area where Ahanu's tribe lived.

The governor had gone off again without giving any indication of what his intent might be toward us. Yesterday, Mr. Lovell told us that the governor had returned, determined to finally take action.

The Reverend Burroughs finished his reading. He joined Mr. Corey and Mr. Proctor in a corner. The Reverend Burroughs seemed nervous, jittery. Mr. Proctor was agitated. As he spoke to Mr. Corey, he became more so.

The Reverend Burroughs moved away from them and began a new verse, something about death. I didn't pay attention to him. I watched as Mr. Proctor moved to my left and Mr. Corey to my right.

I stood and took a couple steps back.

Mr. Proctor rushed to intercept me and grabbed my arm. His other hand wrapped around my throat. He squeezed until Mr. Lovell gripped his wrist and twisted it back. He gave Mr. Proctor a good hit on his head with the baton.

"New governor's returned," Mr. Lovell said. "Given the order to shackle you all to the wall so you don't fly out and torment no one."

He dragged Mr. Proctor across the jail to a far corner and locked him first. The chains were attached to the wall and about five feet in length. They allowed very limited ease of movement.

"Wouldn't want anybody tormenting anybody," he said.

Next, he dragged Mr. Corey to the opposite corner and chained him. Goody Corey was next. He allowed the husbands and wives to stay side by side.

Goody Corey screamed in a manner that made me wonder if the attack on me was her idea.

"She's the one true witch. We need to be rid of her."

The Coreys believed that people were good or evil, not good and evil. There was predator and prey in each of us.

Mr. Lovell moved on from there, locking up the inmates, ignoring their protests.

Mr. Lovell shackled me last. He chained me under the window that gives me comfort, allowing me to stand in place, my place. Unlike many others, I could look out.

Mr. Lovell released Mary Black, the African slave, and me from our shackles once an hour in the heat of the day in order to bring a sip of water to each inmate. I didn't take any water to Mr. Proctor or Mr. Corey for the first three days. Mary eventually took pity on them and took over this part of the task for me.

I wondered if, for once in their lives, the English prisoners envied me. I was allowed to stand and to move about when they were not.

Goody Good's moan filled the still, hot air. She rolled to her side and clutched her back.

I called for Mr. Lovell.

"I want Tituba," Goody Good said. "She's the only one who's nice to me. She was nice even before we were arrested."

I was shocked by Goody Good's statement. I thought

over our limited interactions before we came to jail. It was true that I would give her and Dorcas a nibble to eat most of the times I saw them.

Mr. Lovell released my chains. I knelt beside Goody Good and rubbed the soreness from her back.

"Don't fret," she said. "Dorcas came real easy. It will be fine."

I looked around the dirty, crowded cell and wondered if this could possibly be true.

Goody Good gave a worrisome groan in response. She rolled onto her hands and knees to relieve some of the pressure on her back. She lifted her head and arched her spine like a cheetah.

I went to the barrel, pulled a cup of water for her and touched it to her scaly lips. She greedily drank it down.

Goody Good eased herself into a sitting position using me as a back cushion. She rocked herself back and forth in rhythm with her breathing until her laboring became too great. She slid to the floor on her side, rested and then moved to her back and raised her knees.

"What do you need?" Mr. Lovell asked.

"Water. In a bowl, separate from the barrel and clean cloth."

He went to get these items.

The baby was born without complications. Mr. Lovell cut the cord and whisked it away before we even got a good look. Goody Good was not allowed to see or hold her baby. She didn't get those first moments of closeness when the newborn is laid on the mother's skin to drink.

Goody Good's scream was fierce and primal. "Bring back my baby," but the child was gone.

I ran to the bars and shouted to Mr. Lovell. "Please sir, bring her back."

"This is best, Tituba, " he said.

"No. Just for a few minutes."

"I'm sorry." Mr. Lovell exited the hallway door and disappeared into the yard.

I had difficulty bringing my eyes to meet Goody Good's.

"Her?" she asked.

My lips slightly lifted.

I stood at the window. Through it, I could see the roof of the Sheriff's house. Sheriff George Corwin was the son of Judge Corwin who presided over my hearing. Sheriff Corwin lived in a house near the jail with his wife Lydia. Sheriff Corwin signed warrants against us and was the one who seized the property of the accused. I'm sure his father was very proud.

I saw Sheriff Corwin mount his horse at home and gallop up to the jail's entrance. I came to full attention.

"The sheriff is here," I said. A feeling of dread overtook me.

I remembered my mother as she took Yessi's hand when Yessi had wandered away. "Don't step into the path of the tapir when they run full out," she had said. That's how I felt, that I had stepped into the path of the tapir.

All the prisoners turned to face the door, anxiety written on our faces. In a minute, Sheriff Corwin entered the hallway. He looked at our questioning eyes.

"The new governor's commissioned a special court of Oyer and Terminer," he said.

He entered the cell and approached an agitated Bridget Bishop.

Goody Bishop was said to be a purveyor of charms and potions. She might have actually whispered in some circles at one time that she was a witch. But she had been in trouble with the law before—arrested for witchcraft.

"Not me. No witch. Innocent. No confession. Never confessed." I didn't know it was possible to talk as fast as she did when her thoughts were racing.

It was most important at Goody Bishop's first trial that she insist on her innocence. Confession was generally seen as the most trusted evidence of witchcraft. So, this time, she would not tell a lie to save her life. She would not confess. She held firm in the thinking that confession would see her burned at the stake.

"Liars," she screamed. "Lies. Lies. Lies."

At her hearing, the justices trotted in a trio of men who said that some fourteen years before Goody Bishop had come to them in their bedrooms as a specter. Witnesses were seen as the second best evidence against a witch. The men were quiet in the courtroom, offering no spectral evidence. They did not say that Goody Bishop tormented them still.

"Poppets. Never seen one." She shook her head.

One witness said that he'd found poppets, like the voodoo dolls I remembered from Barbados. They were in the walls of a house where Goody Bishop no longer lived. Goody Bishop could not explain how the poppets got there.

Another witness said that she bought bits of lace too small to have any use other than as dresses for her dolls. I looked over at Goody Bishop who still wore the dress she had on the last day of her hearing. It had a small lace collar.

Goody Bishop had become more disheartened than most during her stay in the jail. She could not see a good end for herself. She was a hurricane, first tumbling into bouts of anger and then despair. At the approach of the sheriff, Goody Bishop began to wail. It was a sound like a wounded animal fresh on the spear.

"Bridget Bishop is the first to be tried." The sheriff

unlocked her shackles only to bind her hands.

"No. No. No," she repeated over and over.

"But, she wasn't the first arrested?" Mary Black said.

Goody Nurse came to attention. "Arrested? Who's arrested?"

Sheriff Corwin took Goody Bishop out of the cell. He held her arm and moved her along on unsteady feet.

No one moved. We were all in shock.

"At least it's quiet again," Goody Good said. These were the first words she had spoken since her baby was taken from her.

Dorcas's lower lip quivered. She could feel the tension in the air.

Goody Good sat on the floor and gathered her in. She rocked herself and her daughter.

"Who's arrested now?" Goody Nurse asked again.

I stood outside by the firepit preparing the evening meal. Goody Good had also been released from her shackles to help. She wandered the yard seeking a bit of solitude.

Mr. Lovell and Mr. Ingesson stood at the ready as I first served the meal for the guards before moving on to making the gruel for the prisoners. Mr. Lovell, usually all smiles and kind words, could not meet my gaze. I found that odd.

Mr. Lowell set down his plate and walked to me. He caught my shoulders and turned me to direct my gaze down the corridor made by Federal Street.

At the end of the street was a tall, rocky hill. A cart under the thick limbs of a broad tree in the distance caught my interest. I stopped cooking to study it.

There was a crowd and I was certain I recognized one man. It was the Reverend Parris, his back turned to me. At the last minute, before leaving the hill, the Reverend Parris turned in my direction. It felt as if he sneered at me.

Beyond him, Bridget Bishop was pulled from a cart. Her hands and feet were bound, a sack placed over her head. A huge man in a black hood carried her over his shoulder up a ladder to the strongest branch of the giant tree. He put a noose around her neck and pushed her away. She was hung from a tree on gallows hill. I sucked in my breath in shock. I turned to Mr. Lovell and saw a tear on his cheek.

Goody Good followed my eyes toward the gallows hill. She walked over. Goody Good lowered her head and turned away from the sight. We silently agreed to say nothing. I composed myself and began to prepare the prisoner's evening meal.

I heard a great winged bird caw in the sky overhead, but I could not look toward the bird. My whole body shivered and I could not control it.

28
Salem Town, July 1692

I sweated in layers of filthy woolen clothes. I tugged at the neck of my dress. About twenty-five of the people who had been arrested were crowded in around me, shackled in this one small cell. It was blasting hot and smelly close.

Not an accused witch, Dorcas was left unbound unlike the rest of us for much of the daytime hours. She scrambled a few steps across the floor toward me. Dorcas held out her arms. I gathered her into my lap, regardless of the heat. I smoothed her hair, fingered out the tangles, and cooed to her.

Mr. Ingesson entered the jail, blazing sun at his back. He carried a length of chain. He rattled the bars as he opened the door. This was likely for effect and the Reverend Burroughs moaned in response, highly agitated in his distress.

Mr. Ingesson came my way. I turned my face to stone. I thought I would care more when my time came, but I didn't care. I was ready to have an end to this torment. Dying seemed a better option than continuing to wait to die. But, Mr. Ingesson didn't want me. He forcefully pulled Dorcas from my arms. Dorcas shrieked. Goody Good, who had been dozing, jumped to alertness. She screamed in such a way as to remind me of the girls' tortured screams.

Mr. Lowell came to the cell door with a list and began to call out names. He looked beyond dispirited. If I did not know better, I would have thought that his name was penned on the list. "Rebecca Nurse, Elizabeth How…"

Mr. Ingesson struggled with the flailing child as he

slipped the chain through a heavy loop and shackled Dorcas to the wall. I tried to give her aid, but the guard knocked me back against the wood wall with his foot.

Dorcas wailed in a wild, incomprehensible way. She struggled against her shackles, attempting to pull her little hands through the hole.

"Sarah Good…"

As soon as Mr. Lovell spoke Goody Good's name, she started yelling at him, releasing all the anger she had pent up. "You'll not take me."

Mr. Lovell continued, "Susannah Martin…"

"I won't go easy so you can hang me." Goody Good's face turned scarlet.

"And Sarah Wilds."

Goody Nurse's face went pale as panic set in. "Did she say hang?"

"They hanged Bridget Bishop. I saw. Ask Tituba. She saw it too."

"Hanged. No," Goody Nurse whispered, grasping her throat.

Mr. Ingesson signaled and, in a minute, several more men appeared. They dragged out the five women.

Goody Corey pointed her bony, shaking finger at me. "See what you've done to us," she accused.

I closed my eyes, tilted my face toward the sun and quietly chanted under my breath until I felt peaceful.

We had not heard the outcome of the trials for the five women, but guessed their fate when outside a crowd of distressed, angry, and curious onlookers began to gather on Federal Street.

Someone started a taunt, a chorus. "Hang the witch. Hang the witch."

I stood in my chains and looked out the window.

"What do you see?" someone asked for them all. If I stood on my toes in just the right spot, I could see down Federal Street.

"All five of them. They're just outside on the street, being carted to the gallows hill." I guessed that they had come directly from the courthouse. "A minister follows on horseback. I can't make out who—his head is bowed and he carries a book close to his chest." I soon recognized him as the Reverend Noyes. He promenaded, preening like a rooster, near to the belligerent Goody Good.

Goody Clinton, closest to me at the window, who had been in silent prayer, suddenly yelled out, "Forgive your accusers."

Goody Good heard and answered with a single word. "No."

"Confess that you are a witch," the Reverend Noyes bellowed.

"I am no more a witch than you are a wizard, and if you take my life, God will give you my blood to drink."

The Reverend Noyes was discomfited by this remark. He pulled in the reins of his horse and let it fall back a bit from the cart as the crowd moved down Federal Street.

On gallows hill, they had built a platform with a staircase under the large tree they had used for Goody Bishop—as if expecting the platform to have lots more use. I could just barely see as Goody Good writhed and fought while she was pulled onto it.

The hangman in his black hood put a cover over Goody Good's head. Her hands were bound, but she kicked at him with her feet. The hooded reaper pushed Goody Good from the platform. Sarah Good was hanged.

The crowd stood there for a moment of stillness and

silence. I did the same. I wanted to let go of my anguish for Goody Good, but could not. She had grown to mean more to me than even Goody Osborne. Now both were dead and gone.

I heard later that Goody Good muttered to the hangman. "If I were a witch, I'd curse you all and your ancestors as well."

I hoped that she was a witch.

29

Salem Town, August 1692

It had been nearly five months since my arrest. I could see my bones through my slack and gray skin. My dry eyes were difficult to open and close. I batted my lids to try to bring some moisture back to them. I touched my face and my hand came away red from my bleeding gums. My hair fell out by the fistful.

And I felt weak. I sat in my spot under the window. I got up to prepare meals, but let Mary distribute the water in the afternoon. Otherwise, I languished in my chains. Days had turned into weeks and weeks into months.

The moon had not completed its full rotation since the last time the guards appeared at the entry to the cell with a list. They massed in force. The Reverend Parris stood at the fore.

I looked at him with pure hate.

He looked at our thin and ragged appearance with surprise, but soon collected himself to his purpose.

"I've come to set you free," he said. "I offer you absolution. Who wishes to save their soul?"

Goody Clinton raised a hand to the Reverend Parris.

I curled into a ball on the floor and turned my back to him.

Mr. Ingesson began saying the names. "George Burroughs…"

As four constables forced their way into the cell. Mr. Ingesson unlocked the chains of the Reverend Burroughs and he came out swinging. His first strong blow handed on Mr. Ingesson's chin, splitting his lip and drawing blood. This caused me to sit up and take notice. I could not suppress a grin.

At the same time, a constable released Mr. Proctor who joined the reverend in the fight. They were of a mind to escape. Perhaps a prearranged plan. The Reverend Burroughs was burley and Mr. Proctor was a tavern keeper, meaning he likely had to rout a drunken person or two in his time.

The Reverend Burroughs landed another good strike on Mr. Ingesson's nose that knocked him to the ground. He dragged Mr. Ingesson the short distance to Goody Proctor who attempted to gain Mr. Ingesson's keys, but a guard that I had never seen before was upon her. Soon, it was mayhem.

Once, Mr. Proctor tripped and fell upon me. I pushed him away. Into the fray. Into the arms of one of the constables.

I wondered about me. What would I do if they won over the guards and Goody Proctor unlocked my chains, something I was uncertain she would do. Would I run away or would I stay for trial? I was still pondering this question when six very angry guards quelled the uprising. The Reverend Burroughs and both Mr. and Goody Proctor were taken away.

Goody Proctor was returned later that day. She was convicted of witchcraft, but after she revealed herself to be with child, about three months along, her hanging was postponed until after the baby was born. We had all heard the making of this baby, grunting from him and moaning with a sound more like pain than joy from her. I guessed Mr. Proctor had found a way to protect his wife, although I doubted that was his purpose.

There was a ruckus going on outside the window. It was another hanging day. I didn't bother to get up and look.

Mr. Lovell unlocked the door and came into the cell. He stood at the window close to me. "Quite the show out there today," he said to me.

"I don't care."

"The Reverend Burroughs made such a fuss at his trial."

"Have they hanged him yet?"

"Unusual for a minister to be named a witch, much less named head of a coven. The reverend, he has friends who do not believe in his guilt. His supporters sought to rescue him."

Mr. Lovell slid down the wall next to me.

"A man's out there on a horse. He brandishes back the crowd yelling, 'He is no minister.' Says it over and over," Mr. Lovell informed me.

I rose with some effort, as I knew Mr. Lovell wished for me to do, and gazed out the window. I saw a man on a horse agitating the crowd.

"I've seen that man before," I said as I returned to my spot on the wall. "That's the Reverend Cotton Mather."

"Heard of him," Mr. Lovell said. "Seems real invested in the hanging. The Reverend Burroughs screamed his innocence and then recited the Lord's Prayer in its entirety. Still hung him. Said it real well too. Something I was told a witch couldn't do." He shook his head. "They keep changing the rules,"

I turned to him.

"Death count is up to sixteen," he said, "if you count the four who died in custody for other reasons."

"Like Goody Osborne," I said.

"Yes," he responded. He looked like he was debating adding to his comments.

"What?" I asked. "What do you wish to say?"

"You know Margaret Jacobs?" he said. "She's a sweet girl, been in the jail since May."

I shook my head no. She was not in this jail and I had not known her before.

"Margaret Jacobs accused the Reverend Burroughs and her grandfather too." He rose to his feet pulling me up with him and pointed to another man who hung next to the Reverend Burroughs from the gallows. "Mr. George Jacobs, Sr."

"If she is an accuser, why has she been in jail these past months?"

"They arrested her anyway. Margaret confessed and then at her grandfather's inducing, she retracted her confession. That's likely why they were both sent in."

"Confessing helps to keep you alive," I said. "No one who has confessed has been to trial, much less hanged." We all knew that.

"Margaret Jacobs refused. She's a person of extraordinary character. In fact, two days ago she confessed to lying when she named the Reverend Burroughs and her grandfather. Said she was tormented by her conscience. Said she choose death with a quiet mind."

And yet five people, including the Reverend Burroughs and Mr. Jacobs hang from gallows hill.

I sat on the floor, pulling at my chains. I covered my head with my hands.

30
Salem Town, September 1692

Before he was imprisoned in April, Mr. Giles Corey was an elderly man of means. He was happy to tell anyone who asked. He was happy to tell anyone who didn't ask. Money was all he cared about. Finding someone else who cared about his money seemed to him to be his best hope of release. He expected to buy himself and his wife freedom.

He was surprised to have languished in the jail with the rest of us for four months. He was more surprised when his day of reckoning arrived. At his inquest, he listened as his accusers confirmed the testimony they presented at his initial hearing. When asked to enter his plea, Mr. Corey would not. Mr. Corey refused to go on trial.

And so he was returned to us.

Mr. Corey returned from his inquest with a story of Rebecca Nurse's sister, Mary Easty.

"Goody Easty and I were taken to trial on this day," Mr. Corey began.

Over the past months, Goody Easty had sat beside me in her chains. Against the wall, she made frequent use of pen and paper. I asked her once what she wrote and she said, "letters, mostly." She didn't seem interested in sharing her efforts with any of us, so I let her be.

Frequently, she did crowd next to me to speak with her kin out my window. They shared events and rumors with her so that she might better understand her situation. This I appreciated.

"Goody Easty was supposed to go to trial a month ago," Mr. Corey said, "but her minister in Topsfield, a Mr. Capon, spoke for her. This caused much debate and her trial was delayed. Goody Easty has written a petition," Mr. Corey informed us, "apparently not her first."

"What did the petition say?" asked Goody Clinton who sat on my other side.

"Goody Easty wrote about how the proceedings were mostly against women who weren't able to plead their own cause. Nor was the testimony to her good character from people like her own Mr. Capon taken into consideration. She wrote about the weight given to the acting out of the accusers and suggested that reasonable precautions must taken against the testimony of witches or those afflicted by them."

At this moment, Mr. Lovell returned Goody Easty to our company and her chains. He had heard the end of Mr. Corey's account and was curious to hear the rest.

Instead, Mr. Corey paused to let Goody Easty take over.

Goody Easty tried to adjust herself into a comfortable position. She propped herself against the wall and struggled with the heavy links.

"You don't see it from in here," she said, "but everybody is accusing everybody. The accusers name people not just from Salem Village and Topsfield. It's spread widely, especially in Andover, all over Massachusetts really."

"Oh," Goody Clinton said, a silent tear slipping down her cheek.

I leaned closer to Goody Easty and the conversation, interested like the others.

"There are too many," Goody Easty tried to appear calm, but she raised the pitch of her voice. "And now they reach too high. They name high-ranking people. The courts tried to ignore charges against the wife of the Reverend John

Hale or Judge Corwin's mother-in-law. Change is looming. It must come."

"Tell them the terms of your petition," Mr. Corey said, but continued before she could. "She said the girls are wily in their accusations. She said she appreciated the aspirations of the court, but that too much innocent blood had been shed."

"Appreciate the aspirations of the court," Mary Black repeated, bitterness in her tone.

"She made two recommendations," Mr. Corey said.

"What?" a half dozen people asked in unison.

"I suggested keeping the afflicted persons strictly apart from the confessing witches," Goody Easty said. "To see if they could tell the same story. To find the truth."

Goody Easty had made good use of her time in jail. She seemed reasonable and right-minded to me. No doubt keeping the accused apart from the accusers would have made a difference for most all of us.

"She implied that some of the confessors had lied," Mr. Corey said.

"They likely all lied," Goody Black responded.

"I did not wish to anger the magistrate. I had to carefully select my words," Goody Easty replied. "More than forty people have confessed, but none who have confessed have been brought to trial."

"So what was your other suggestion?" Goody Hobbs asked.

"She suggested that they begin trials of people who have confessed."

"They struggle under the weight of so many confessors. Their power diminishes by ignoring those confessions."

Mr. Corey was puffed up. Proud. He hadn't confessed. Many people listening hadn't confessed, but I had. Just the same, it wasn't me who let out the cry of alarm.

"Why? What were you thinking? I don't want to die," Abby said. Abby was a young girl and had her whole life in front of her, if she lived through this.

Forty people had confessed according to Goody Easty, but I didn't know most of them. There was Goody Hobbs and her stepdaughter, Abby, and me. These were the three people I knew, who lived with me in this jail.

"So many people rushing to proclaim that they are a witch. 'Thou shall not suffer a witch to live,' Exodus 22:18. That's what the Bible says," Goody Easty answered. "If there are truly witches, they should be put to death, but it is my thinking that the claims are fraudulent. They must be made to prove a witch or let us go."

"That's why I refused to enter a plea," Mr. Corey said almost reverently.

Sheriff Corwin came for Mr. Corey.

"That's my finest suit," Mr. Corey said.

"I cut a fine figure in it too," Sheriff Corwin said. He strutted a bit.

"You can't seize my property. I have not entered a plea."

"Your stubbornness will serve you little on this day," Sheriff Corwin said.

Three days later, Sheriff Corwin returned. He didn't look quite as dapper. Dirt clung to the sweat on his brow and his hands showed many small cuts. He grabbed up Goody Easty and Goody Corey and dragged them out the door.

As I was preparing the evening meal, I looked down the length of Federal Street. Eight people hung from the gallows. Seven were women and I believed I could make out the figures of Goody Easty and Goody Corey. There was one man. I did not think him to be Mr. Corey, but from this distance I couldn't be sure.

"Goody Easty and Goody Corey?" I asked Mr. Lovell when he came for his plate.

"Yes."

"Will Mr. Corey return to us?"

"No."

Mr. Lovell was usually much more expansive in his words, but not today, so I encouraged him. "What happened to Mr. Corey?" I asked.

"It was horrible," Mr. Lovell said. "They lay him on a board and stacked boulders on him. Sheriff Corwin insisted that he enter a plea, but Corey said he would not. He would not stand trial."

"So the Sheriff added more stones?"

Mr. Lovell nodded. "For two days. Corwin tortured him and Corey stayed mute. He never gave in, although he did cry out in pain until he could no longer get air into his lungs."

"Is Mr. Corey much injured?"

"You misunderstand. He's dead. He was pressed to death. They threw him into a rocky crevice on the side of the hill. They didn't even toss some dirt on top. They didn't give him a decent burial."

Mr. Lovell was much affected.

"We're travelers, my people. My grandfather was hanged along with most of my Romani relatives, so my father left Scotland. My father was shot in Nova Scotia, so we came here." Mr. Lovell took my hand. "I hate this place with all my being. It's time for me to move on." He paused for a moment.

He was saying that he didn't wish to die here. Neither did I.

"You could come with me?" he asked.

Some of the prisoners had whispered that Mr. Lovell

had favored me in his treatment, but I had refused to see it. He offered me an escape from the fear, the pain. He offered to take me away from the constant anxious boredom. I wanted that, but he also offered to release me from any possibility of John or Violet. But hadn't I already given up John and Violet. Wasn't that my sacrifice? Wasn't it likely I'd never again see the ones I loved again? I thought about the strength of my love for my family in a way I never had before.

My head was still swimming with possibilities when Mr. Lovell released my hand. He kissed my cheek before he left.

31
Salem Town, October 1692

The weather had cooled off. Goody Parris visited for the first time. Her health seemed improved from when last I saw her, unlike my own. I was weak and disinterested in all that happened around me. I did not bother to rise to greet her.

Goody Parris brought my blue shawl to me. She wrapped the shawl around my shoulders and I held it tightly to me. Goody Parris smiled in recognition of the cheer she knew it gave to me. As she left, she bid me look out the window.

I heard the sound of familiar laughter outside. I thought I was mistaken for a moment, but then I heard it again. I struggled to my feet and looked outside.

Betty, Abigail, Elizabeth, and Ann stood in a row.

"There she is," Abigail said.

All the girls' happy eyes turned toward me. Betty waved a little. They moved in a mass toward the window. I could here scuffling and giggling.

In a minute, Ann, tallest of the girls, appeared at the high window. She stood on a wooden box left nearby for just this purpose.

The inmates, who had been listless and vacant until Ann appeared, met her with jeers and angry remarks. Someone threw a shoe at her that bounced remarkably far.

Ann signaled for me to come closer to the window and I did.

"How are you feeling, Ann?" I asked warily.

"Better. Much better. We all are." Ann nodded her head

toward Betty who had taken a few steps away from the window with the other girls to watch us. "Betty has been away with relatives. She is just returned."

"She looks very well indeed." And so she did. Much recovered.

"Betty says to tell you that she misses you. She wanted to be the one to speak with you, but she was too short."

I wanted to wait to hear the purpose of the girls' visit, but I had to know. "Do you see my baby and John?"

"John was sick, but he's doing better as well."

"And Violet?"

"John keeps her secreted away as much as possible, but she seems in good health when we see her." Ann responded to what must have been distress on my face. "Maybe he will visit soon."

"No." I didn't need her feeding me false hope. We both knew he could never travel to Salem Town.

"He loves you a great deal. He pines for you," Ann said. "Everyone says so." She sighed, a long protracted breath. "William has gone from me for good. He does not speak to me. Fortunately, he refuses to even look at Mercy. He has a new friend. He spends all his time with him."

I wished to chuckle despite myself, but I could not.

"Mercy's moving to Boston in a month or two," she said. "Have a fine trip, I say."

There was a long silence while I waited for her to find her point.

"I guess the right witch has been hanged."

Someone behind me, but within earshot, hissed at Ann.

"Why?" I asked for us all.

"I was hurting. I just wanted it to stop. I did what I was told."

I thought about end of summer. The rye that made the

girls sick would be gone. A new crop grew in the fields, waiting for a fall harvest. I wasn't so unwise to think that people would simply feel better and wake up to what they had done, but with the tainted rye gone, I felt an eerie moment of hope.

"I feel that Satan deceived me to bring about innocent blood. I was stupid and I wanted to say that I am sorry. I don't believe that you are a witch," Ann said.

A true confession. Maybe the first of the trials. Contrition and repentance with the wish to do better.

"That thinking is a bit late," I said, not yet ready for forgiveness. "Who told you to say our names?" I hoped for another true confession, but it did not come.

Ann hung her head. She fished in the pocket of her garment. She drew out a small package.

"We wanted to bring this to you. Abigail fished it out of the fire."

Ann handed the bundle to me. She stepped down from the box, but stopped and climbed back. "I think you should recant. Others are," she said.

I opened the bundle to find my zemi on a new length of leather rope. The girls had found a few chicken feathers and sewed them on for ornamentation. In my mind, I could see them working on it. With love.

For the first time since this all began, I cried. I put the charm around my neck. I began to tuck it under my dress, but thought better of it and let it fall visibly open.

That night I dreamed.

I hovered in the air near the sky place. I could see everything from where I was.

The Taino shaman painted serpentine lines onto his torso. He led the Barbados slaves as they performed a surreal dance. The dance intensified and dyed the sky around me amethyst, the color of wind.

The Arawak shaman from my childhood tribe looked up into the clouds. He waved his hands and shouted at the heavens. He used all his strength to fling the evil spirits away. We made eye contact. He opened his mouth and crows flew out. The crows disappeared on the purple wind.

The full moon cast eerie shadows that climbed the walls. I startled awake from a restless sleep. My clothes were soaked with sweat from a fever dream.

The guard who had replaced Mr. Lovell had removed our chains. If anyone in charge had known that we were released, they didn't protest. My wrists were raw and red, but mine were not the worst. We all needed the open air to heal our wounds.

All around me were sleeping prisoners, except for one other inmate. Martha Sparks was awake. Goody Sparks was younger than me. She had a husband who had gone to fight Indians in the east and she hadn't seen him in quite some time. And she also had a father, her daddy, who came to see her frequently. He brought her food, blankets and paid for extra straw.

Goody Sparks pointed to a barrel.

"Bring me a cup of water," she demanded of me.

Goody Sparks was wearing down my last bit of patience. She was as close to the water barrel as me. The incessant sobbing in despair stopped without Goody Bishop. The room wasn't so loud without the rants of Goody Good. But the void was filled with Goody Sparks, who lorded over me as if I were her personal slave.

I rose to my feet and walked over to the water barrel. I stared into its murky depths. Blackness. Emptiness.

John's special power was silence. I asked him one time what was my special power? He said that my power was disguise, like the walking stick or leaf butterfly that appeared like their surroundings. I had the ability to appear exactly as expected, to say exactly what someone else wished to hear.

With that one exception.

Mr. Lovell was the only one who had been genuinely kind to me since William Porter and his father brought me a blanket in the Ipswich jail. The Porters didn't know how I still clung to that blanket for warmth and comfort.

The men of Salem Village thought that power came from money, land, and servants. For the most part, I had always known what the men of Salem Village thought of me. The Reverend Parris stood on the pulpit and told anyone who cared to listen what to think about slaves.

But it was the women like Mrs. Pearsehouse, Mrs. DuVille, and even Goody Sibley who distressed me. They had position in the community and money. Plus, they had the force of their own personality to give them power. My mother had this power. It came from her spirit animal—the songbird. She could use the power of her voice to make the men hear her. I had seen Salem women use their voices for other purposes—to help themselves. But never to help me.

I thought about my dream. I believed the message from the shamans was that they wished to share their power with me. I did not need to perfectly perform the African or the Taino or the Arawak ceremony. I needed to cast out the evil spirits through my own curing ritual of my own device.

"You think I should be quiet," I said to Goody Sparks. "A compliant slave even as a prisoner of your hate."

I pulled a scoop of water and poured a cup.

"You think I should do for you."

I took a sip and then poured the remainder of the water into a circle on the floor. I bent the metal handle from the cup until it broke off. I pulled some straw together into a pile within the wet circle.

"In all these years of looking like you, acting like you, I have never forgotten who I really am."

I pulled off my cap and let loose my hair. I ran my hands through my hair until I had half a dozen long black strands. To the straw, I added a bit of rat's nest I found in the corner.

"I don't believe in your God of death," I said.

I removed my zemi necklace. The zemi was made from flint stone, curved flat at the edges. In my thoughts, I called the Zemi God of Protection. I used the edge of the stone to repeatedly peel a layer of iron from the cup handle until it warmed and then ignited a spark. I burned a bit of the straw over the wet floor until I had a small pile of ash.

"I believe that there is a benevolent spirit in all living things. I believe that the loving and peaceful spirits can be called upon to protect us from the angry ones."

I pulled off my dress and stood in my shift. I used the char from the ash to paint serpentine lines on my face and arms.

"I believe dreams are visions into the future. And my dreams tell me to dance."

I chanted and danced in the light of the moon.

Much to my surprise, Mary Black rose to her feet and followed my actions. She began to dance. More inmates awoke and looked on with startled eyes.

"What are you doing?" Goody Clinton, who had been in jail for almost as long as me, asked.

I had recognized Rachel Clinton when she was brought into the jail last March. She was from Ipswich. I had gone with Mrs. DuVille to deliver a hat to a patron in that town and Goody Clinton had followed us on our errand, hands stretched out for a donation of food or money. Goody Clinton was a beggar.

"Calling peaceful Indian spirits to protect us," Mary said.

Goody Clinton shrugged her shoulders and scrambled to her feet. She joined the chant and dance. A few others also danced. They laughed at their efforts in the dark.

I swayed from the effort, dizzy, in a self-induced trance and then I yelled so I could be heard in the sky place by the grandfather.

The other dancers stopped short.

"What was that?" Mary asked.

Goody Sparks scoffed. She sat alone and unyielding on the floor.

I screamed and used all my power and strength to pitch away the evil spirits from the jail.

On the other side of the bars, in the corners where the room was most black, a man watched from the shadows.

"Are we safe now?" Mary asked.

A well-dressed man entered the jail. He smiled and pressed the hands of the prisoners to which he spoke. He chatted for a moment with each one.

He approached me.

"And your name is Tituba?"

I nodded.

"I'm Sir William Phips, Royal Governor of the Bay Colony."

A second man brought a chair on which the governor sat. He was an elegant man, calm with a reassuring smile. I was bewildered.

"That means I am," he paused as he searched for the words he wished to use, "the chief of this tribe." Governor Phips pointed to the second man. "My associate here is a very religious and learned man. He's studied and traveled a great deal. He tells me you are from Barbados.”

“For a short time.”

“And before that, somewhere off the coast of South America. You’re Arawak?”

This word was familiar, but I said nothing.

“My friend, he’s been to these places, met other slaves like you. He helps me prepare a report on the subject of the witchcraft trials in Salem. Tell me your story, Tituba Indian. Tell me what happened to you.”

“It’s near eighteen years past.”

He waited expectantly.

I was surprised at his curiosity. In all my years with these strange pale folk, no one had ever asked a serious question about my past.

The governor listened to my story. After I finished, he looked sad as he sat in silence for a moment.

“My man says that you are a smart woman, a strong woman, a compassionate woman, but you are not a truthful woman.”

“I’m a living woman.”

“You said at your hearing that you were a witch.”

“My family is safe because I have said what I was told.”

“What do you mean?”

“The examiner, he would say what he wanted and I would say it. He would say, ‘How many people?’ and I would say a number.”

“You made the number up out of your head.”

“Yes sir.”

“You said what you thought the judge would want to hear?”

I nodded.

“What I want to hear right now is the truth.”

Again, I nodded.

"Are you a witch, Tituba Indian?" he asked.

"I'm not a witch, sir."

"You recant?"

"Yes sir."

"What do you want most at this very moment, Tituba?" he asked.

"What I have wanted since the start of this. I want my husband and my little girl to be safe."

Governor Phips nodded. "I understand. That takes a great deal of character—to want for them, not yourself, after so many months fearing for your own life in this cell." He leaned in close. "Shall I tell you a confidence?"

I was startled, but leaned in to hear.

"My wife has been named as a witch. I'm not sure I can be so brave."

32
Salem Town, December 1692

There were fewer people in the jail. Inmates were called for court dates and never seen again. We didn't see them on gallows hill and so never knew what became of them.

The Reverend Parris entered. He gestured for me to come to the bars, but I didn't move. He yelled at me from across the room.

"Tituba Indian." His voice boomed.

Still, I didn't come forward.

"You may have heard that the Governor has pardoned you."

I hadn't heard. None of the prisoners had. They lifted their heads in interest.

"Pardoned you all," he said. "So, if you can pay for your upkeep these past ten months, you may go." He turned to me. "I won't pay your board. I won't have you in my home."

"How much do I owe?" I asked.

"I've sold John Indian," he said.

"To whom? Not to that wilderness man? Who's got hold of my husband? Is Violet with him?"

He stopped and turned. "We are at an end, you and I."

I ran to the barrier and grabbed his clothes through the bars. I held the lapels of his jacket and the white of his collar with my last remaining strength. The move shocked him into temporary silence as his rage grew. But not more than mine.

"The grandfather sent you to a rich place with fish in the sea and game in the woods. He sent you natives to show

218

you how to grow and harvest the plants, but you and your family starve in this land of plenty."

Mr. Parris pulled my fingers from his collar. It hurt as he bent them back, but I held on. "You are the demon. You are the confessed witch." His face was blood red as he spit the words into my face, but I did not flinch.

"You call yourself a spiritual leader without bothering to learn the old ways and so He sends you a test. Do you love and protect your people? No. You hang them from a tree. "

"You will never leave this cell. You will never see your family again."

"My shaman shows me the blessed way, the peaceful way, even here in this hateful place."

Mr. Parris backed away from the bars. He held his head high, but the image he projected was false.

"This is your tribe." I indicated the prisoners in the jail. I could see their eyes on me, listening to me. "Do you think these people will follow you when they are released from jail? Do you think they will pay your parson's fee? Do you believe anyone will?"

He slapped me hard right through the bars.

"I believe your children were sick and you used them for your own gain. Someone whispered in your ear. Goody Putnam?" I speculated. "I've heard rumors that she has yelled witchcraft before to further her own purposes."

He pulled himself free of me, stomped down the hall, and fumbled with the outside door.

"These people," I looked at all the people who surrounded me, "think of slavery as a result of life's misfortune or a plunder of war. They have never seen you buy or sell a human being for your own personal gain. Until now. But I have."

The prisoners thought for just a moment about the

reality of John and I living among them. I saw it in their eyes.

"I have a theory. Do you want to hear it? I think you know that you can no longer be the minister of Salem Village. I think you know you must find a new way to support your family. I think you target those who will not pay your wages. I think you and the Putnams sell the accusations of the children for a fee?"

I ran to the window and screamed after him as the Reverend Parris escaped the jail and stormed away. "But, you failed. Again. Like your failure with your father's plantation. Like the failure of your shop. You will die disliked and penniless."

I sunk down the wall and smirked. I felt good.

Outside, I heard a buckboard. All eyes turned to the jail door.

"That's my father," Martha Sparks said. "He petitioned the governor for my release. He stood before the court and guaranteed a bond. Today, I am to be released."

"With no trial?" I asked.

"No trial."

Goody Sparks's family members entered the door and stood at the bars. Mr. Ingesson was with them, keys jangling from his hand.

"I can't wait to see home," Goody Sparks said.

Her father shook his head. "Your farm was taken long ago. I had to sell everything else to effect your release."

"Where shall I live?"

"Not in Salem Village," he proclaimed.

An elegant man in a fancy suit entered the jail. He looked lasciviously at Mary Black. To my shame, I did what I could to hide in the shadows. I pulled my shawl over my head.

Mr. Ingesson collected a large number of coins. His pockets were weighted down with them. He entered the cell and roughly pulled out Mary Black.

She struggled to no purpose.

Dorcas Good's father came for her. He took Dorcas's hand and led her out of the cell.

"You'll be learnin' better than your mother," he said.

Dorcas turned to look back at me. She waved.

I tried to smile for her sake.

It was down to the two people who had no one. Goody Proctor remained with me. All of her belongings had been confiscated and Mr. Proctor had made no provision for her in his will, likely thinking she would be hanged as well. In many ways, Goody Proctor was now poorer than I was.

When I heard the sound of a wagon pulling up, I clamped my eyes tightly shut.

Mr. Ingesson came in and gestured to me. He led me out the jailhouse door into blazing sunlight. I blinked in the light of day. I struggled to stand unshackled, alone in the sun. I raised my face to its rays and closed my eyes. Spots of yellow and orange light dotted the inside of my eyelids.

When I opened my eyes, I saw Mr. Ingesson handing down Juliet DuVille from her carriage. She counted six coins into his palm. Mr. Ingesson took the coins and went back inside.

I walked to her.

"Welcome to my household, Tituba. You are sold to me. My fine ladies still clamor for your colorful weaving."

I heard pounding, the sound of hammer on boards. Beyond this reunion, the hangman pulled down the platform from under the tree on gallows hill.

Mrs. DuVille turned to her conveyance.

"Ma'am," I said. "I'd like to walk on my own."

Mrs. DuVille smiled. "Of course."

She climbed aboard, flicked the reins, and the horse and carriage ambled away.

I removed my cap and let down my hair before I followed behind.

33
Boston, March 1692

Mrs. DuVille had redone a small area of the workroom for me. There was a little bed in my space, the first I'd ever had. When Mrs. DuVille wasn't entertaining, she sometimes took tea with me. These niceties confused me.

Mrs. DuVille added feathers to a hat she was in the process of making.

I stopped the weaving I was doing to watch her.

"You've been very nice to me," I said.

She gave me the gift of a slight smile.

"Am I still a slave?" I asked.

Mrs. DuVille looked disconcerted. "I did pay your fines from the jail," she said. "Maybe after that is paid off, we could talk about a different kind of arrangement."

I had made two shawls, a blanket, and four baskets since returning to Mrs. DuVille. I had seen many more than the six coins she gave to Mr. Ingesson put into her own hand.

"I paid the Reverend Parris for you." Mrs. DuVille looked lost in her thoughts. "And there is still your room and board to consider."

So, I was still a slave.

"I heard that John was sold by the Reverend Parris. Do you know anything of him?" I asked.

"He was sold." There was something she did not wish to say. Something she felt conflicted about. I could see it in her eyes, but finally she decided to speak.

"John has run away," she said. "No one knows where

he's got to."

His new owners had searched for John and did not find him. They did not know where John was. Mrs. DuVille did not know where he was. But I did.

Tomorrow, I would pack a basket and go to find Ahanu, his lovely wife, and the People of the Dawn. John would be there and I hoped Violet, too.

The End.

End Notes

Tituba, a native of an Arawak-speaking tribe of Venezuela or Guiana, was presumably captured by Captain Peter Wroth on the English ship *Savoy*.

Rye was a common New England crop.

Ergot grows on grains like rye during warm, damp and rainy weather. The conditions were right for ergot in the growing seasons before the witchcraft trials in Salem in 1692.

The effects of ergot are cumulative with prolonged exposure.

Ergot poisoning is characterized by symptoms including: crawling sensations in the skin, tingling fingers, vertigo, headaches, muscle contractions and hallucinations. Salem villagers who may have experienced these symptoms would have had no way to understand them.

Thomas Putnam, Jr. was a large property owner who paid the rates of the reverend and the doctor in rye from his farm.

When the tainted rye was gone and a new crop had replaced it, the afflicted people got better.

There was nothing extraordinary about charges of witchcraft to explain the unexplainable in that time period. Reports indicate five persons were executed in Massachusetts prior to the Salem trials.

No single factor can explain what instigated or encouraged the witchcraft trials. It was a culturally, socially and politically complex time.

Over 150 arrests were made in Salem in 1692 and 53 people confessed to witchcraft. In total, 24 people died: 19 people were hanged, one man was pressed to death and four people died in custody of other causes.

It is not known what happened to Tituba or her family after she was pardoned.

The Reverend Parris, faced with possible dismissal from his post, addressed his parishioners and apologized, admitting that he "erred and offended." He attributed his blame to Satan.

In the summer of 1697, the Court of Common Pleas gave The Reverend Parris his salary arrears in return for resigning his post and vacating his claim to the parsonage.

In 1706, Ann Putnam, Jr. wrote out her confession to being a part in bringing about innocent blood and had it read out to the parishioners in Salem Village.

As the historical record is sparse in some ways, some characters are totally fabricated in this story. These include Mrs. DuVille and the specifics of Tituba's Arawak family.

I used multitudes of books, articles and websites about colonial life, South American natives and Native Americans in the New England area, slavery and the Salem witchcraft trials. These four works most inspired my interpretation of events.

1. Caporael, Linnda R., Ergotism: The Satan Loosed in Salem?, Science, Vol. 192, 2 April 1976
2. Breslaw, Elaine G., *Tituba: Reluctant Witch of Salem,* New York University Press, 1996
3. Rosenthal, Bernard, *Salem Story: Reading the Witch Trials of 1692*, Cambridge University Press, 1993
4. Salem Witch Trials:
   http://www.salemwitchtrials.com

About the Author

Nancy Smith is a freelance writer of novels (*The Slow Kill, Tainted Harvest*), screenplays and short stories. She is also a filmmaker, script analyst, and script supervisor. Nancy is the owner of First Look Script Analysis, operating since December 2005 and First Look Publishing operating since 2016. She lives in Austin, Texas.

http://www.nancysmithwriter.com
https://www.facebook.com/nswriter/

Please write a comment on Amazon:
http://www.amazon.com

Also by Nancy Smith

THE UNIVERSAL VACCINE

A science fiction mystery

Seventy-five scientists working on a universal flu vaccine are murdered. Who killed them and why?

University of Texas art student, Isa Vedkka, comes home to find police on her doorstep. They tell her that her microbiologist mother and engineer father as well as all of her parents' coworkers are dead. Isa wants to understand what happened. She enlists the assistance of investigative journalist Rory Burke to find out. The pair have no idea where this search will take them.

Coming Soon.

THE SLOW KILL

A near-future science fiction novel.

After years of drought, famine and disease, botanist, Frank Harvey, brings hope with his project to build a water pipeline and hydro-farm over the cracked, barren lakebed that is Austin, Texas' water supply. Frank's aim is to deter evaporation and protect his hydrofarm, but his big boss at the Wagner Company locks and electrifies the gate of the dome, forcing Frank apart from his wife and six-year-old son. Frank must find his son and demonstrate to him that he is not abandoned, but loved.

"A cautionary, futuristic tale that balances dystopia with altruism, "The Slow Kill" explores the complexities of human relationships as the characters struggle to survive the hardships of an enduring drought. A clever narrative with vivid descriptions and strong cinematic images. You might call it science fiction, but this premise doesn't stray too far from reality. It really could happen to all of us. And then what?" *Jill Oleson, writer*

"Smith deftly reveals Frank's sense of disconnection, exacerbated by the privileged lives that people live in the dome. As the story intercuts between Frank's and Alex's personal turmoils, there's plenty of timely social commentary, but it avoids ever feeling preachy." *Kirkus Reviews*

www.ingramcontent.com/pod-product-compliance
Lightning Source LLC
Chambersburg PA
CBHW071152170626
46809CB00002B/869